SPEAK OF
THE DUKE

TAMARA
Gill

COPYRIGHT

PROLOGUE

J ulia inwardly groaned when she spied Lord Cyrus Franklin, Marquess of Chilsten, heading her way after speaking to her newly minted brother-in-law, the Duke of Derby.

Why he was making a direct line toward her was anyone's guess, and she could only think of one. The marquess knew the monetary amount of her dowry and wanted to meet one of the sisters not yet engaged.

Well... She steeled herself to be cold and aloof. After all, this was not her Season to even look for a husband. She wasn't even out yet, so his lordship's needing to speak to her was nothing more than a man looking for a rich bride.

She would not be his rich bride, that was for certain.

She knew all about him and his rakish past...or present. Really, she ought to amend. The gossip rags of London printed nothing but Marquess of Chilsten's nights of revelry and vice. The rumored lovers whom she had heard whispers of the moment she stepped into this very ballroom.

That he was the duke's friend was unfortunate and not something she could change. But that did not mean she had to be welcoming of his address.

"Mrs. Woodville, I know this is very forward and untoward of me but would you do me the honor of introducing me to your daughter?" he said, grinning at her mother as if that would make any difference to Julia. She couldn't care less that he was one of the most handsome men in England. His reputation was atrocious, and the last thing she wanted was to marry a man who broke her heart a month after saying their vows.

And he would break her heart. No man as wicked and wild as he would change his ways to suit a woman. Even if that woman was his wife.

"Lord Chilsten, may I introduce you to my daughter, Miss Julia Woodville." Her mama smiled as if she were doing Julia a great favor, but she could not see it that way. She saw a wolf, ready to pounce on her and leave her brokenhearted in his wake when he was through with his little diversion.

She would not be a diversion for him. Not if she could help it.

"Lord Chilsten, it is very nice to meet you," she said, her tone one of boredom and one she hoped he would understand soon enough.

His smile looked forced, and she inwardly crowed that he had picked up on her cue.

"Would you care to dance?" he asked her, looking at her mama. "If your mother does not mind?"

Julia shook her head, speaking before her mama had a

chance. "I'm not dancing this evening, my lord. But I'm certain my refusal is another lady's crowning moment, do you not agree?"

His eyes widened, and instead of being shocked by her words, he grinned, throwing her completely off course. She clamped her mouth shut, not needing to see how handsome his grin made him look, even more devastatingly good-looking than when he was merely smiling.

"Perhaps another time then," he said, bowing. "If you'll excuse me."

"Of course," Julia answered, watching with not a little bit of pride as the wolf walked away, tail firmly between his legs.

"Julia," her mother scolded, digging her fingers into her arm. "Why would you deny such a catch a simple dance? You should have obliged him. Do you not know who he is?" Her mother looked back to where Lord Chilsten had walked as if she already missed his presence.

Julia did not, nor did she care. She shrugged. "No, why would I know who he is or any of these people? It is not like anyone has gone out of their way to befriend me. I'm not even out yet. I should not be here at all."

"You are old enough to attend a ball, even if you have not made your curtsy to the queen. But that is the Marquess of Chilsten and future Duke of Rothes."

"He's going to be a Scottish duke? That would explain the wildness that so obviously runs through his veins."

Her mother gasped, shushing her. "Whatever has got into you, child? Why would you say such a thing about his lordship?"

"Because it's true, Mama," she answered. "Do you not read the society pages in the paper? They are always talking

3

of Lord Chilsten and his wayward lifestyle. Anyone who marries his lordship should brace themselves for heartache, for he will not keep a wife well pleased for long. Not if what they write about him in the papers is true."

Her mother paled a little at her words. "I have read the stories, but we do not know that they are true," she defended him.

"Do we not?" Julia nodded in the direction where she watched Lord Chilsten talk with another lady guest. Their conversation she garnered by the lady's lascivious pout was much less innocent than the conversation he had with her. "Look, Mama. Look at him now. Why, if I were to lay some of my pin money down, I would say that his lordship is trying to woo his way into the widowed Dowager Duchess of Barker's heart right at this minute." And woo his way under her skirt. Not that she was that forward with her mama, but it was so obvious to anyone with eyes what he was doing.

Julia had little doubt that his lordship would leave with the Dowager Duchess of Barker or someone else. Whoever fell for his false charms and seductive wiles.

Her mama glanced in his lordship's direction. "Well, I never," she said as Lord Chilsten picked up Her Grace's hand and kissed it, lingering over her fingers for longer than was proper. "Mayhap you are right, my dear. We will look elsewhere."

Julia smiled. "My thoughts exactly," she said, determined not to look in his disgraceful direction again for the entirety of the ball.

. . .

Cyrus leaned against the window, watching the delectable Miss Julia Woodville as she warded off suitor after suitor who bowed before her precious silk slippers asking for an introduction or dance.

The woman never lost her sweet visage, even when the words that spilled from her lips seemed to satisfy the men she was denying while also cutting them off at the knees. He shook his head, unable to fathom how she was doing it without them all knowing what she was actually doing. And yet, her mother's less-than-pleased visage told Cyrus that at least when it came to her mama, the woman was not fooled by her daughter's actions.

His eyes slipped over her form. A tall meg, that was certain. She had come up to his nose, and he was over six feet himself. Many men bowing before her had to look up at her to meet her eye. It was odd to see a woman towering over most of those in attendance.

Not that Cyrus minded that so much. The thought of her long legs wrapped about his hips as he pleasured her left him aching to study her in a more private setting. Her wit and veiled insults had not dissuaded him. No, indeed not. If anything, they made him more curious to learn what it was exactly that Miss Julia Woodville would look for in a gentleman admirer.

Why she did not like him. Not that he needed to really think too hard on that matter, if truth be told. He knew his reputation proceeded him. He was a rake, a legacy he had earned from both his parents, who had remained married but had numerous lovers coming and going from both their country estates and London homes. Oddly enough, their marriage had been a contented one, and he could not fault them for their choice if it made them happy. Even if that meant he most likely had a bevy of siblings he did not know about.

He took a calming breath, thankful that his own legitimacy had been verified and his name and homes could not be taken from him. His parents had been less than proper when courting, and Cyrus knew their marriage had only occurred days before his birth. He thanked God every day his grandfather had forced the marquess to marry his daughter or face him on a field at dawn.

He sipped his drink, his eyes following her as she excused herself from her mama. He expected her to head for the door that led to the lady's retiring room, and at first she did, but then, glancing over her shoulder and noting her mama's attention was not on her person, diverted toward the terrace.

Cyrus pushed off from his post and followed her, wanting to see where the chit with the viperish tongue was going. Mayhap she was meeting an admirer that no one knew of. The thought made his steps increase. Why he could not fathom. He had only just met the chit, and if she could find a husband who wanted a traditional marriage, then all power to her.

Even so, he followed close on her heels. He looked along the terrace, not seeing her admiring the gardens, but then he spotted her blue silk skirts slipping around the corner.

He smiled, following to catch her out for whatever she was up to. The minx Miss Julia Woodville was a lady with secrets, and he could not wait to uncover them and mayhap use them to his advantage.

. . .

Julia strolled along the darkened terrace, pleased to be alone at last. She pulled out a cheroot from her reticule and lit it using a wall sconce that burned nearby before moving farther into the darkness to where a lone seat sat against the wall. She breathed a sigh of relief for the first time that night as only the muffled sounds of the ball sounded far away, and the stars were her only company.

Being here this evening was an absurdity that her mama ought to have denied. She wasn't even out yet, and already she was exhausted from the society with whom she had to circulate. Her coming out would be as far from her lifestyle at Grafton as living on the moon would be.

Her gaze wandered upward to the bright, circular shape far up in the sky, and she studied it, wondering if it had valleys and mountains similar to those on Earth. Footsteps nearby pulled her attention away, and she looked toward the direction she had come, only to see Lord Chilsten strolling her way.

She stood, needing to face him and not be subservient to his presence. There was something about the man that put her on guard. Not only his infamous reputation but something she could not put her finger on. He made her wary, and she did not like the fluttering in her stomach whenever she viewed him.

He was the last man any woman in London wanted to marry. She wasn't even certain she wanted to marry at all, not unless her love for her prospective husband outweighed all her reservations and concerns.

She had never found it easy to trust people she did not know for a particularly long time, so making a match within three months or thereabouts during a London Season seemed almost impossible.

"Miss Julia," he said, chuckling slightly when he spied her cheroot held between her two fingers. "Well, let me start by saying I did not think I would ever see a debutante outside a ball smoking. An oddity indeed."

She finished her cheroot, throwing it onto the lawns where she knew it would do no harm. "And you still have not, my lord, for I'm not yet out and therefore not a debutante."

"Touché." He strolled past her and sat on the bench. Feeling oddly tall with him seated, she joined him, looking out onto the grounds. "I must say, Miss Julia, please do not take offense, but you are extremely tall. Are any of your sisters still in Grafton as tall as you, or are you the only one blessed with such length?"

She raised her brow, giving him a displeased look. "I'm the only one. Well, the only one who is taller than my parents." She paused. "Is there any other reason as to why you've followed me outdoors, my lord? It seems very odd, not to mention ill-advised, considering I'm unchaperoned."

"No one will come looking around here. I'm confident we're safe enough."

Julia fought not to sigh. She had not wanted company on her sojourn outdoors. She wanted five minutes to herself. To be alone without the cloying smells of sweat and perfume and the incessant gentlemen who thought to talk their way into her heart. "And if I did not want you to join me? Do my wants and needs not factor into your conscience when this is what you want?"

He narrowed his eyes, and she noticed their color was such a dark brown they could almost be termed black. Being so dark, one would think they would be soulless, but they were not. They sparkled with mirth and interest. Mirth

8

she could stomach. The interest that burned in his eyes was a waste of his time.

"You do not like me very much, Miss Julia. May I ask as to why?"

"Why?" she replied, wondering where she ought to start. "You have a terrible reputation. You are written about in the paper almost weekly with some escapade or scandal. You are rumored to have numerous lovers, all of whom are married women to other lords, and you are as far from what a lady would look for in a husband as one could get. I know you're friends with my brother-in-law, the duke, but that does not mean that we can be or that I will allow you to believe you have a chance at winning my hand, for you do not."

His mouth gaped before he threw back his head and laughed. Julia stared at him, seeing his smile that literally took her wits from her. She stifled a sigh of wonder at his beauty. The man was a rake, a rogue, a sinner of the worst kind, but oh dear, she could see why women would sin with him. He was wild and carefree and did not care what people thought. Certainly, he appeared to relish the scandals that society wrote about him.

"I am no more interested in your hand in marriage than I believe you are in gaining mine, but I find you charming in your own prickly way. And there is nothing I like more than a challenge."

She raised one brow, trying her hardest to stare down her nose at him. "I'm not a challenge you'll win, my lord."

He tipped his head, shrugging. "I think you may be, even if that challenge is not to secure your hand, but merely a kiss. You are disillusioned by the prospect of marriage, and after watching you this evening, I'm certain of this fact."

"You were watching me?" she asked, aghast to learn he had been. What had he seen? What did he surmise from keeping accounts on her?

"Yes, I watched you a great deal, and I noted that while you're very polite to prospective gentlemen, you do not show any interest besides that of a woman meeting a person she will never see again after the fact."

"And you're going to change my opinion on men and make me more interested in what they have to say? How will you do that, my lord? You're not a magician."

He chuckled. The low and gravelly sound made her body thrum in places it ought not. "I do not think you've experienced passion enough to know what the opposite sex could offer you. If you allowed me to kiss you, to show you what us mere men of the world can make you feel, I think it will only help you decide what is best for you when you make your curtsy to the queen next Season." His devilish grin almost pulled one from Julia's lips. Almost. "What do you say, beautiful? Are you willing to test my theory, or are you too frightened?"

His last word was not what she appreciated. If she were one thing in this world, it was not frightened. Not of anything and certainly not of him. The pompous, self-loving popinjay. "Very well. I shall allow you to kiss me. Once. And then you may leave me alone for the rest of the evening." Let him try to show her what men could make her feel. He would fail, and she would revel in her triumph.

He nodded. "Agreed."

Cyrus took the opportunity to study Julia's beauty, a beauty that had pulled his attention from the first moment he happened upon her. Her skin, unblemished and perfectly English, shone under the moonlit night. Her full lips beckoned him in a way that others never had before.

He cradled her face in his hands, tipping up her chin to make her look at him. She stared at him with a boldness that suited her words. Deep in his soul, he knew this woman did not lie or deny herself anything she wanted. He did not want to refuse her a thing either.

He lowered his head toward her, watching as her eyes fluttered closed, her long, dark lashes fanning over her cheeks. His gut clenched, and he swallowed the fit of nerves that followed. So damn beautiful that it wasn't any wonder that his heart stopped. He brushed his lips over hers. Soft and malleable, she opened for him, giving him the ability to kiss her as she deserved.

"You're so beautiful," he whispered before kissing her with more force. Her small sigh as their lips touched and fused made his body hard. He wanted this woman in his arms. He wanted to kiss her until the early hours of the morning. Never go back within the bounds of the ballroom walls and be separated from her touch.

Cyrus frowned, unsure where such thoughts came from. The feel of her tongue slipping over his lips caught him unawares. He held the nape of her neck, his other hand tipping her head back farther to deepen the kiss. She was sweet, luscious, and bold.

Their tongues tangled, and the kiss changed. Altered. No longer was it an example of what she could have with another man. The man she would eventually marry. No. This was a kiss from a man who desired the woman in his arms. A kiss one gave a lover before thoroughly bedding them. Inappropriate and scandalous, a kiss he could not stop and did not want to end.

Her hands settled against his chest, judging the muscles

beneath her palms. Her little murmur of delight told him she liked what she touched.

"I could eat you alive," he said, kissing her hard, devouring her mouth as if his life depended on her kiss. Her fingers gripped his hair before her arms went about his neck.

Images of them abed, of her wild and fired hot from his touch, bombarded his mind. He wrenched her onto his lap, his hand slipping from her waist to mold her breast.

She undulated against him, pushing into his touch, seeking more. He gave her what she wanted. Hell, what *he* wanted. His cock, rigid in his pants, craved her heat. He wanted her, here and now.

Stop, Cyrus. She's innocent.

He fought for control, to rein in his desires. He could not take a virginal miss, but damn it all to hell, there was something spectacular about the one in his arms.

He had thought her prickly and cold. She was anything but. She was all soft curves and ample flesh. Her kisses rocked him to his core and made him as hot as Hades.

He slipped the bodice of her gown down, sliding his finger over her pebbled nipple. She gasped, and the kiss turned molten, fast and wanton. She pushed into him, and his back came up hard against the house's stone wall, and he groaned.

"Julia," he begged. "You're a seductress who'll haunt my dreams."

"You tease as well, my lord," she gasped.

"Cyrus. Call me Cyrus, please," he begged of her.

Her wicked grin almost undid him. "I cannot return to the ball having spent in my breeches. You must stop, for I do not have the power to do so."

"Stop what?" she asked, all innocence. "I thought it was

you who was to show me what I could have with a husband?"

He laid his hand over her hip, stilling her movements. He took the opportunity to feel her thigh and work it beneath his fingers. "I'm sure you're an educated woman who's read books and does not need me to explain in any further detail what should happen if you keep rubbing against my cock." Her eyes flared at his crass speech, but she did not flee. On the contrary, she grinned, raising one brow.

"Whatever do you mean will happen?" she asked again, moving once more against his manhood. He clamped his jaw shut on the expletive he wanted to shout out. He was a marquess, for God's sake. The future Duke of Rothes. Not a man who came in his breeches after an interlude with a virginal debutante at a society ball.

She's not even a debutante, you dunce.

"Do you not like how I make you feel?" she asked him, placing small, quick kisses against his lips.

"It is me who is supposed to be showing you what it is like to have a man kiss you. Show you how pleasurable the mouth can be when joined with another."

"Hmm," she sighed. "I think I know now what you're referring to in this little game, my lord. I do think you have won."

He clasped her hip, helping her undulate against his cock. He wanted to come, to find pleasure from her even if that meant that he would have to leave. He would see her again. There would be other nights to seduce her away.

The Season was young, after all. "Kiss me again," he begged her, feeling his balls tighten. She did as he asked, the force of her embrace snapping his head against the wall. He came, hard and long, groaned his release into her mouth like a green lad during his first time with a woman.

She kissed him as the last exquisite tremors settled through his body. "Actually," she said, pulling back and meeting his gaze. "I think in this game, we have both won. Do you not agree?" she asked him.

He nodded, fighting to keep his bearings. "I do," he gasped. Determined that this would not be the only time they were together. Not if he could convince her otherwise.

It was not over between him and Julia Woodville. Not by any length.

CHAPTER
ONE

The Season, 1807

Miss Julia Woodville, some would say, was the most fortunate young woman in London, for the Season of 1807 had been a triumph indeed. She had two sisters overlooking her debut, the Duchess of Derby and Viscountess Leigh. Two gently bred country girls who had landed themselves at the top of the Haute *ton*.

It was not an easy feat and not one that Julia wanted to aspire to, no matter how much her mama wished it. Unfortunately, it was also something that her sisters seemed incapable of understanding too.

She stood out on the terrace, remembering another night such as this but a year ago. Had it been so long since she had enjoyed a night of revelry?

Guests mingled indoors and out at her sister the Duchess of Derby's London home, which, although they called it a town house, was anything but that. It was a mansion and took up a good portion of Berkeley Square. The Georgian house exuded money, wealth, and power, and now she was part of that world. The expectations on her were immense, and she wanted none of it.

Why could she not have been able to marry a fine country gentleman when she was ready to marry at all? The London gentlemen were fickle and liars, a certainty she knew very well already.

Julia glanced down the terrace, watching society at play. All of them were scheming and spoke of what they assumed the other person wanted to hear, not what the actual truth may be.

This game they played during the Season was not what she had envisioned for her twentieth year, and yet, here she was, expected to marry Lord Ronald Howard, Viscount Payne. She did not love him, even if she did like him very much, and that was the rub. Would her family wish her to marry if she only liked the gentleman? Disappointment ran through her like poison. Although she had never aspired to marry, now that it was expected of her, she did at least wish to marry a man whom she loved and who loved her in return.

Not to fall at any rake's feet which would lead one down a path lined with disappointment and hurt.

"Miss Julia, here you are. I have been searching all over."

The familiar voice of Lord Payne sounded behind her, and she schooled her features before turning and smiling in welcome. "Lord Payne, you have arrived. Tardy as ever," she mentioned, knowing he was over an hour late. Something he was famously on time for as always.

His cheeks reddened, and she wondered where he had been before arriving at the ball. "Apologies, Miss Julia," he said, bowing a little. "I lost track of time at a previous event, but alas, I am here now. Should we go back indoors and do a turn about the room?"

She nodded, proceeding him and trying not to flinch when he took her hand and placed it on his arm. Several guests threw them knowing glances. She discerned what they were thinking. That Lord Payne and herself would soon be announcing their engagement. They would not be, not if she could avoid it.

They came up to some of their mutual friends. Julia moved to stand beside her best friend, Reign Hall from Grafton, who had come up to London to debut with her. Where Julia was tall, Reign was of normal height and had a lovely golden hue to her skin. Julia had always been jealous of her sun-kissed skin since she always believed herself to be so pale that she would disappear if she were ever to step before a white wall.

"I see Lord Payne found you, Julia," Reign stated, watching his lordship with boredom that Julia often felt when around Lord Payne. She did not want to be so hard on him, for he was kind and tried to be affectionate, but there wasn't that spark that she wanted there to be between them.

A spark brought to life by a rogue the year before.

She closed her eyes and fought to remove the memory of Lord Chilsten from her mind. The rogue had fled to Scotland not long after their kiss and married some Scottish woman no one had ever heard about or even seen. He did not deserve a moment's thought at all.

"He did locate me," she answered, clearing her throat, trying to remove the boredom that chased her every word. "I do not know, Reign," she whispered, pulling her friend away to ensure privacy from those of their set. "I know he's asked Papa for my hand in marriage, and Father has agreed so long as I agree, but I do not feel anything for him."

"Nothing at all?" her friend asked, with compassion in her blue gaze.

Julia shook her head. "Nothing but benign friendship, and I want to feel more than that. The way my sisters and their husbands look at each other whenever they think no one is watching them is what I want in a marriage. I want passion and love, and well, I know I will not have that with Lord Payne."

"Maybe if you let him kiss you. You know," Reign whispered, leaning in close. "Like you allowed Lord Chilsten. Maybe if you kissed him too, things would be clearer. If there is no spark, you know he is not for you."

Julia cringed. Not wanting to kiss his lordship at all. And she was certain that should she allow such liberties, he would be all but assured her heart was his, and he would make an offer of marriage. No, she could not do it.

"I cannot. The thought of doing such a thing with his lordship makes my stomach churn in the most unlikeable way. No, I could not test that theory with him." Not that she could test it with anyone. Not really. She thought back to her night with Lord Chilsten. As much as she had stated to his face that she disliked his lordship, and she certainly did not approve of his conduct or reputation in town, she had wanted to kiss the rogue. And what a kiss it had been.

One she had dreamed about for weeks afterward. Whenever she closed her eyes, she relived the feel of his muscular chest, his heart beating fast as they kissed and he found pleasure in her arms with a recklessness that still left her aching.

What if she never found that with someone else? What if she only ever reacted so with a man who was no longer on the marriage mart? A man who had married and disappeared to Scotland.

If that occurred, she would do her duty and marry a man she liked above anyone else, even if there was no charged emotion between them.

"If you feel so strongly against Lord Payne, you do need to discuss the matter with him and allow him to choose another. If your skin crawls at the thought of kissing his lordship or even bedding him, the marriage will be a disaster."

"I know," Julia sighed. "I will discuss the matter with him, and soon. I merely need to pick my moment."

Reign patted her arm before she took two glasses of ratafia from a passing footman. "Here, let us have a drink."

Julia sipped the sweet beverage, staring out over the sea of heads, an ability she and only a few other gentlemen as tall as she were capable of doing. "Have you seen Lord Lupton-Gage is here this evening? Have you forgiven the marquess yet for splashing mud on your gown at the park the other day?" she asked her friend, keenly watching her reaction to hearing of the gentleman's presence at the ball. As much as her friend had protested at the disgraceful act that Julia still was not sure he knew he had done, her friend seemed overly engaged with a man she had never met before. Enough so that Julia could not help but think Reign secretly admired the marquess.

"I have not," Reign protested, her eyes darting all over the room as if searching for the man of whom they now spoke. A welcome reprieve for Julia, for she did not want to speak of Lord Payne any further, nor think of the Marquess of Chilsten.

"He is across from us, speaking to my sister, the duchess," Julia offered, sipping her drink to hide her smirk.

Reign's mouth flattened into a displeased line. "Oh yes, there he is," her friend growled, and Julia laughed. "I shall not rest until I have become even with the man. He ruined my new walking gown Mama had paid extra for it to be made quickly. I shall not forgive him."

"I do not think he saw you when he ran through the puddle. If you remember, you were behind those small bushes hiding from Mr. Riley and merely stepped out from behind them at the most inappropriate time."

Reign glanced up at her, her eyes wide with hurt. "You are not defending him, are you?"

Julia shook her head, dismissing the notion from her friend's mind. "Of course not, but he is very handsome and well, to be introduced and to mention what had happened at the park is a good way to start a conversation. Of course, if you are inclined to think the same way as me."

Reign chewed her lip, and Julia looked back to where Lord Lupton-Gage stood with her sister, except now his attention was not on her sibling but on her friend. The interest in his lordship's eyes was not hard to see, for Julia had seen similar when she had first happened upon Lord Chilsten.

The memory of him made her heart ache. Any woman would have presumed just as she had that after the sort of kiss they had shared, more would follow. That he would have—no matter her protestations—pursued her to see what may be, if anything.

But he had not. She had not seen him again, and then she had read of his marriage in Scotland over breakfast a month later.

Could it have been a year already since that night? It was hard to fathom in all truth, for it felt as though it happened only yesterday. Never in her life had she wished more to be wrong about the notorious rake of London, but it would seem she had not been. He had moved on from her without nary a thought and married someone else. That she supposed was something for she could not see him marrying anyone unless he loved them, so the woman who became his wife was likely one he loved very much and one who had stolen a rogue's heart.

Reign gasped and clasped her arm, shaking her a little. And that is when she heard it, the other startled murmurs of the *ton*, the whispers and excitement from certain ladies who stood nearby.

Julia glanced toward the door, and everything within her turned to stone. She felt her mouth gape in shock, and she shut it with a snap, schooling her features as quickly as possible.

It could not be. She did not need him back in society, not when she was trying to find a husband who ignited all that he had within her.

"Lord Chilsten is here. Do you think he brought his wife?" Reign asked, her eyes as wide as Julia knew hers to be.

"I do not know. No one has ever heard of or seen her before. Maybe he has," she replied. Lord Chilsten bowed before their hosts, kissing the duchess's gloved hand before glancing about the room as if looking for someone.

The pit of her stomach clenched, and she held her breath.

Waiting.

Hoping.

You're a fool, her mind mocked.

And then their eyes met across the ballroom floor and she knew, right down to the silk slippers on her extremely long feet, that he had been looking for her.

Julia jumped as the high-octave voice of Lord Payne spoke beside her. "Oh, would you look at that? Lord

Chilsten has returned, and I see he has not brought his wife with him. Not surprising considering his history."

Julia glanced at Lord Payne, or at least glanced down at him. "You believe he left her in Scotland?" she asked, looking back to Lord Chilsten, but not seeing him with her sister any longer.

"Oh, I do not doubt it. He may be married, but I do not think he would care for the union. It is long known at the gentlemen's clubs and society at large that he never wished to be tied down to anyone. I will admit to being quite shocked at the reading of his marriage. No doubt there is scandal attached to it. No marriage of Chilsten's would be anything but associated with that word."

Julia took in Lord Payne's words, but maybe his lordship was wrong. Mayhap Lord Chilsten had fallen in love. That at least gave her some comfort since the thought of such a thing made her all but green with envy.

"Miss Julia, we meet again," the deep, gravelly voice ran over her like water, rejuvenating her parched heart after a long drought.

She dipped into a curtsy and glanced up at Lord Chilsten. She had forgotten how very nice it was to look up and not down at a gentleman with whom she conversed or danced. And certainly, this man who made her long for things she could never have.

"Lord Chilsten, it seems that we do."

He smiled, and she ached in places no lady ought to. For so long, she had wanted that feeling again, and to have it with a married man was not what she needed or wanted.

Damn it all to hell. And damn him for marrying anyone, especially since it was not her.

CHAPTER
TWO

Cyrus drank in the sight of Julia Woodville after a year of not seeing her. He knew that she would attend the Duke and Duchess of Derby's ball and his being here and happening upon her was not by chance. Not that she would have him, nor would any of the ladies present, for that matter. Not when they found out the truth as to why he'd been absent from society for the past year. All of them would go running to their estates and close their polished doors in his face.

But Julia Woodville was the only woman he wanted to seek out, and dance with if she agreed. He knew he could never make her fall in love with him, he was a rake, and his absence from London was only more proof of that, but he had to see her again. Drink in the sight of her, if only from afar.

The poxy Lord Payne beside her looked at him as if he were not the marquess and future Scottish duke, but a bug squashed beneath his feet and it irked. His lordship was merely a viscount, and if he needed to remind him of that fact, he would do so. He may live a life of vice, of debauchery, but he'd be damned if he allowed anyone to look down their noses at him or his family.

"Has it been a year since we have conversed? I can hardly believe it," he said, ignoring Lord Payne, who frowned down his long nose as if he'd swallowed something sour. More's the pity that he had not.

Miss Julia smiled up at him, seemingly pleased at his presence. "I have not seen you since my sister the viscountess's ball, my lord."

Her voice floated over him like a balm. He had tried to remember how she had sounded during all the long, lonely nights of the past year in the wilds of Scotland but had never been able to form the sound in his mind.

Hearing her again left his heart to race. "We conversed, if memory serves me correctly, on the terrace. Is that not so, Miss Julia?" he reminded her. Remembering that night all too well.

"I do not think such outings wise, Miss Woodville," Lord Payne interjected, frowning at Chilsten. "A lady should never be unattended with a gentleman. You do yourself no credit, my dear."

Chilsten frowned at the endearment. My dear? Were the rumors true that Miss Julia Woodville would soon be betrothed to Viscount Payne? Surely not. Looking at them, he had to admit they did not suit. Certainly, she was a good foot taller than the man, not to mention she looked less than pleased by his opinions on her conduct while at balls and parties.

"Our discussion was nothing untoward, Lord Payne. Do not suggest otherwise," she said, her tone a good one or two degrees colder than it was before.

He watched Miss Woodville, noting the rosy hue forming on her cheeks. He knew better than anyone that their interlude on the terrace, the side terrace, shadowed in darkness from inquisitive eyes, was anything but untoward. It was scandalous. Ruinous and utterly worth repeating if he could get her alone at any time.

"Hmm, well, I do hope so," Lord Payne said, blind to the fact that Miss Julia did not appreciate his concern or his insinuation. "The future is dependent on many things, which I'm sure you wish to protect as much as I."

"Do beg my pardon, Payne, but you talk as if there is an understanding between you and Miss Julia. Is that so? Have I overstepped my mark here?" he asked, seeing no reason not to seek the answer directly. He had never been a man to sit and wait when wanting to know something, and he did not see why he would start now.

Payne's face blotched red, and he stumbled over his words while trying to form a reply. "I would never presume, of course, but as with any lady at such events, propriety and etiquette must be followed."

"How very boring," he stated, smiling when Julia chuckled and covered her mirth with her gloved hand. "Will you dance with me, Miss Julia? It has been too long since I had you in my arms."

Payne choked. He could only presume what Cyrus's words meant. Chilsten took Miss Woodville's hand, leading her onto the floor as the first notes of a minuet started to play. "I do apologize for speaking out of turn, but your beau is frightfully annoying, and I wanted to madden him as much as he vexed me."

Miss Julia lined up beside him, taking his hand. "You should not tease him so. Lord Payne is very kind, a little simple at times, I grant you, but he is agreeable to me."

"And that is what you want. A husband who is simple

and agreeable?" he asked her, meeting her gaze. "Why not just get a puppy?"

Her lips tightened into a thin line, and she shook her head, a pretty curl dropping to her shoulder and making his mouth dry. "No, of course not. It is merely one of many things that I look for in a husband."

"He's absurd," he blurted. "You would be bored within the very first moments of taking your vows, and as for your wedding night, well," he shuddered, hating to imagine such a heinous act, "I do not think it would be worth your while."

"If I recall correctly, Lord Chilsten, being in your arms for more than five minutes was not worth my while."

Her words halted his steps, and Lady Cole crashed into him. He apologized and quickly fell into the step of the dance once again. "A kiss," he whispered, "is not the same as taking your wedding vows and being promised to someone until death do you part. And in any case, your time in my arms was certainly worth my while."

She shrugged one delicate shoulder and his gaze settled on her perfect, unblemished skin. He wanted to kiss her again. Be so close to her as to smell her scent that he gained wisps of even now. Jasmine and something that was uniquely her teased his senses. Hell, he wanted to drink her in, smother himself with her so that he would forever have that memory.

"I will admit that our time together did give me a notion of what I was looking for in a husband as you promised it would. But since then, I have found little to interest me, so the venture was a waste of time," she said.

Did that mean she did not find Payne desirable as much as she had found him desirable? "You mean," he said as they moved through the dance. "I sparked something within you that you've been searching for ever since? Something you have not been able to find?" He threw her a wicked grin and chuckled when she raised her chin in defiance of his words. "I'm more than willing to give you a repeat lesson if you have forgotten any part of our...chat."

Her mouth settled into a displeased line. "No, thank you, my lord. I have no interest in a repeat lesson and certainly not from you. Your reputation has degraded further since you left England, in my opinion, in any case. It is scandalous for me even to be dancing with you." She met his eye, pinning him with a hardness he had not seen before. "Where is your wife, my lord? Rusticating in Scotland so you may enjoy your freedoms here?"

Cyrus knew what he was about to say would shock and hurt Julia, but there was no getting around the fact. The truth was the truth, and by tomorrow, all of London would know. "She is dead, if you must know," he stated, watching the blood drain from her pretty face. "I have returned for the Season a widower, and if that is not scandalous enough, my good friends, the Duke and Duchess of Derby invited me this evening. There will be no getting rid of me from your society so fast, Miss Julia. Even if you wish it."

Her gaze slipped over him, and he felt every moment of her inspection like a physical touch. He'd been too long without a woman. No matter what society thought, or the rumors that followed him back from Scotland, he was not as scandalous as he once had been.

He had a daughter to think of now, and he would do all he could to ensure she was accepted into society, even if her parentage was a little shadowy. To return as the rake he once had been would not help in that happening, nor would his choosing a wife who was not a powerful voice in society, enough to enable his daughter to enter it like the lady she would one day be.

He would find the right woman to be his marchioness, a woman who was both rich and powerful from birth. When he found that lady, he would ask for her hand and secure his daughter's future.

Miss Julia Woodville was not that woman, for all her beauty and impressive dowry. He had promised himself to have her in his arms one night before letting her go forever. But nor would he allow her to be married off to the boring fool Payne. That would never do either.

"Why are you back then, my lord? Should you not be in mourning?" she asked, looking about the room so she would not have to look at him.

He flinched at her words, hating the barb behind her question. He ought not to be here. The death of the marchioness was not twelve months past. When London found out he was back before a respectable mourning period, his reputation would be once again believed before anything else.

"I needed to return to my estates in Sussex," he lied, knowing he had solely left Scotland because he could not stand another day not seeing the woman who danced in his arms right at this very moment. That he had heard rumors of her impending marriage and had to be near her again before he lost her forever.

Julia stopped in the middle of the ballroom floor, staring up at him as if he had sprouted a second head. He pulled her from the dance to the side of the room. "Are you going to faint, Miss Julia? Should I fetch some smelling salts?" he asked, not liking the paleness of her skin. "Say something, anything. I'm sorry to have shocked you." And he was. He had not meant to make her swoon with the horror of his words.

"You ought not to be here. You're in mourning. While I understand that you need to attend your estates, attending a ball is wrong," she said, chastising him, and rightly so.

"It was sudden and unexpected, and nothing could be done for the marchioness. Please do not feel sorry for me. I do not deserve your sympathy." And he did not. His wife had cared for him as much as he had cared for her, which was very little. But he had not wanted to see such an end for her. Never that. He could only hope now to give their child a better future than her shaky beginning.

Julia watched him a moment, and he felt her scrutiny to his core. "Either way, you have my sympathy, my lord. I'm sorry for your loss."

He nodded, wanting to end the discussion. His dead wife only caused him shame. He deserved people to look down on him, in truth. He had lain with one of his servants and had gotten her with child. A scoundrel thing to do and so like him. At least he had married her and given their child legitimacy, if he could do nothing else. More than his father had ever done for any children he had sired around England.

Cyrus looked out onto the room, anywhere but the misguided concern in Julia's eyes. "I have returned to London to find you most favored. A diamond of the first water and a much-sought-after young lady," he commented. "And you're telling me that it was only with myself that you felt anything at all. Come, Miss Julia, that will never do. We must find you a gentleman who will spark your desire." He leaned close, wagging his brows at her. "I know you have it. I've experienced it myself."

She rolled her eyes, and he could not like her more if he tried.

"You have no idea what you're talking about. I tested a theory with you, nothing more. Do not read into my kiss any more than that."

Oh, but he did read into it more than he ought. It had been one of the most honest but intoxicating kisses of his life. A kiss with a woman who was not trying to leverage herself in society or name him as one of their conquests. She had not been trying to gain anything by his touch, and he'd known the moment their lips touched, there was no malice in her. That did not stop him, however, from wanting more of her.

Even now, when he ought to leave her alone, let her marry a man who was as good and pure of heart as she was, he did not walk away. She would hate him when she knew the truth of his sudden flight to Scotland when she found out that he was a father. That his wife was once his maid, not some respectable lass from a noble Scottish family, which they all presumed.

So far, he had kept such information from the *ton*, but it was only a matter of time before everyone knew, and then he would be ruined. Few would invite him anywhere then, and as rich as he was, he knew his marriage would not be as grand as he needed it to be.

Still, he could not walk away from Julia. He liked her too much to do the right thing.

"I would like us to be friends," he said, never having said truer words. "No matter our shared history, our paths are certain to cross in this society. I would much prefer you an ally than an enemy."

She stared at him, almost nose to nose, and he wondered what her quick mind was thinking. Her eyes narrowed a little in thought before a slight relaxing of her brow told him she had come to a decision. "Very well, we can be friends."

He grinned, bowing as if meeting her for the first time. "Cyrus Franklin, Marquess of Chilsten at your service, Miss Julia Woodville," he said, taking her gloved fingers and kissing them. "It is a pleasure to meet you properly this time. I look forward to our friendship."

She pulled out of his hold, shrugging one delicate shoulder. "So, what will our new friendship encompass?" she asked him.

"Well, as for that," he said, leaning close. "Since you're determined to find a great love match, mayhap that is something I can assist you with. You have no brother of your own to guide you, correct?"

"No, I am one of five sisters," she answered.

"Well then, let me be of service to you. I promise not to lead you astray...again," he teased.

Her lips twitched, but now she looked at him with interest, not as if he were a wolf about to devour a sheep. As much as he would like to devour her, he would not. If friendship enabled them to be near, that would suit him well enough. And when the *ton* broke the news of his scandalous actions in Scotland, mayhap Julia as his friend would stand by his side.

He hoped.

CHAPTER
THREE

J ulia looked forward to the Edwards's ball the following evening. She knew that Lord Chilsten would be there, and she wanted to discuss the matter of Lord Jackson, who had sparked her interest earlier in the Season before he left for his country estate for matters she had not yet discerned.

In any case, he was now back and as popular and handsome as he was before he left. Many young ladies gathered about him at balls and parties. He was tall and dark-haired, had a friendly face that looked innocent, and there was less gossip about him than Lord Chilsten.

Her gaze wandered over to where the marquess stood talking to her brother-in-law, the Duke of Derby, and her sister the duchess. Lord Chilsten did not look innocent at all. In fact, he looked as if his face were chiseled from marble, all sharp lines and rigid features. His body, she knew from memory, was as hard as that stone, and she flexed her fingers in her gloves, pushing the knowledge from her mind.

If they were to be friends, and for him to help her find a suitable husband who was not as wild and wanton as he was, she needed to stop comparing everyone to him. He was her friend now, one with whom she had shared a kiss, but a kiss that was for educational purposes only. It meant nothing, and it was unlikely he would be looking for a bride.

But what if he *was* looking for one, and he just had not told her?

Julia swallowed, taking a calming breath when the thought caused her blood to thump loudly in her ears. He would not look at her. After all, they had kissed, and that had not stopped him from racing to Scotland to marry his bonny lass.

No, he would not look at her. He had stated as much the moment he offered to be her friend and guide her toward a respectable match. That alone told her he did not see her as a potential wife. In any case, anyone who was not Lord Payne would do, the man with whom she did not have any emotional or physical attraction.

Lord Jackson was, however, suitable. An earl who would satisfy her mama with numerous properties and fortune. So he would not be chasing her dowry above her heart. A good match, all told.

She bit her lip, watching Lord Jackson musing over the possibility of shifting her attention toward him.

A light shoulder bump brought her musings to a halt, and she turned to find Lord Chilsten grinning at her with a knowing look. "I see lord Jackson has piqued your interest. Would you like me to tell you a little about his lordship?"

She bit her lip, hoping that Lord Chilsten was being true to her and not playing with her in this game of friendship and usefulness. "If you know of anything of his lordship, that would be most informative."

He cleared his throat, glancing at the fellow before meeting her eye. "His family goes back several hundred years to the Norman Conquest. He's an earl and has an income of eight thousand a year. His estates are in Nottingham. He's not as innocent as that baby face would tell you, but he is not as wicked as me," Chilsten divulged, waggling his brows.

Julia shook her head at his antics. "I doubt there are many as wicked as you," she drawled.

He chuckled, the deep timbre of his voice making her shiver in awareness. "There are few who are as wicked as me. But you'll have to kiss him to find out if you have any reaction to the fellow. You know the one," he mentioned, bumping her shoulder again. "Like our kiss that left you all flushed and hot in my arms."

She gasped, not quite believing he would state such a thing to her. No matter how true it was. "You're the devil. You cannot say that to me."

"Why not?" He shrugged. "It is true, is it not?"

She glared at him, only to find herself lost in his eyes for longer than she meant. He had the darkest brown eyes she had ever seen. They were large, almond-shaped, and surrounded by the longest lashes. Was there no end to his beauty? How could one gentleman be blessed with so much good fortune while others were left wanting?

"I cannot go around kissing everyone. My reputation would not survive. It was fortunate that we were not caught last year. But," she added, "I will spend time with him, see if I have any fluttering in my stomach."

"Did you have fluttering with me?" he asked her. "It sounds as if you did."

She rolled her eyes, yet she knew she had felt so with Chilsten. She had felt a longing and need that coiled up tight within her and one she wanted only him to sate. "If I did, it was only nerves from never being kissed before." She took his arm, pulling him toward the ballroom floor. "Come, dance with me. If you're to help me find a suitable gentleman to marry, you can start by dancing with me."

He stared at her but relented, holding her hand against his arm as he led her out onto the floor. The fluttering was back. In truth, it never left her, not when Chilsten was around her person. He had promised, after all, to help her find a suitable husband.

Why that man could not be him, she could not fathom, for it would certainly make her life a lot simpler if he would relent and offer for her. They managed well enough and were becoming friends, which was a good foundation for love to grow.

"Tell me again, my lord, why do we not suit? Not that I'm pining for you, you must understand, but we are now socializing within the same social sphere, and my fortune is enough to satisfy anyone I should imagine."

"Are you always so forward, Miss Julia?" he asked her, slipping them into the other sets of dancers as the sound of a cotillion started to play.

"I suppose I am," she admitted. "You disapprove, I feel."

He shook his head, taking her hand as they danced down the line of couples. "Not at all. I find you refreshing, as you well know, but unfortunately, the complications of my life have made it necessary for me to marry a woman of status, not so much fortune when that time comes. Otherwise, you would have suited me very well. In fact, I think we would have rubbed along quite well together."

His eyes darkened, and she couldn't help but feel he

meant more to his words than he stated aloud. "So if we're determined to marry different people for reasons we may and may not divulge, this comradeship will work splendidly. Maybe even I can be of assistance to you and help you marry a woman not only of high rank but a pleasant mannerism as well. I'm sure you would wish that to be so, would you not?"

"Of course." He held her hand as they skipped around the other dancers before coming back into line. "But in truth, I believe I shall be able to find my bride well enough. You are searching for love, a much more difficult emotion to pin down. It can be as elusive as the sun here in England."

Julia knew that well enough. The many gentlemen introduced to her had been enough to make her head spin. But her heart remained still throughout except with the rogue at her side. The organ always seemed to do a little jig when he was around.

"I have a dance later this evening with the Marquess of Perry. He came up to me at the beginning of the ball and asked me to dance. I could not refuse, and you said there was much to recommend him." He was handsome and well sought after as much as Lord Jackson was. After dancing with him, she would know if he evoked anything other than mild interest in her. She was sure of it.

Lord Chilsten cleared his throat. "Of course," he agreed. "There is much to recommend Lord Perry, and I do not know of any impediment or scandal rumored about the fellow that would stop me from suggesting him as a suitor."

"Do you approve?" she pushed, wanting to hear him say it.

"I approve," he said, throwing her a small smile.

The dance came to a reluctant end, and he led her to the

side of the room. "I shall stand beside you and keep you company until his lordship comes for your dance."

"Oh, you do not need to do that. I have a quadrille with Mr. Watts now and shall not be alone long. In fact," she mentioned, "my dance card is full this evening. I shall have very sore slippered feet in the morning, you may be sure of it."

"Let me know if you're ever in need of a foot rub," he suggested, his tone dipping to that deep timbre that left her breathless.

She shook her head, pushing at his arm. "Stop your teasing. You know how inappropriate saying such a thing is."

"You would enjoy my foot rubs. I'm very thorough."

Julia gaped at the rogue, unable to fathom the idea of such a thing. The idea of a man giving a woman a foot rub did sound heavenly, but she had little doubt in her mind that once he touched her feet, he would be less than satisfied stopping his touch on that location only.

Admit it. You would like Chilsten's hands elsewhere. Just as you dreamed of the last time you were in his arms for nigh on a year.

"You have practiced quite a lot, I'm sure." She raised her brow, daring him to say otherwise. He could not dispute her. The man enjoyed touching women as much as she enjoyed Gunter's Ices.

His mouth twitched as he tried to hide his smirk. "Maybe just a little, Miss Julia," he said.

Just at that moment, Mr. Watts came to claim his dance. Lord Chilsten stepped back, and she smiled at Mr. Watts as he bowed before her. "My dance, I believe, Miss Julia," he said.

She went with him, making a point to touch his arm and see how her body reacted to connecting with his. Nothing happened besides the feel of his lovely superfine coat beneath her gloved hands. Certainly, there was no fluttering.

CHAPTER
FOUR

Julia threw herself into the dance, determined to feel what she did whenever she was around Lord Chilsten with someone else. The man dancing with her was everything she ought to want in a husband, and she was certain if he showed an emotional interest in her, love could blossom from such a start.

"You come from Northamptonshire, I understand, Miss Woodville," Mr. Watts stated, watching her keenly as they went through the dance steps.

"I do. Grafton, in fact. Have you ever been?" she asked him.

He shook his head, his lips pinching as if he'd tasted something sour. "No, I have not had the pleasure," he answered, his tone the opposite of what his words suggested.

Something inside her seized at the notion he disapproved of her somehow, or most certainly where she had grown up and loved. "You look as if you do not like Northamptonshire. Is there something about Grafton that you know, and I do not?" she asked him, holding his gaze.

A light blush rose on his cheeks, and she narrowed her eyes, wondering if he would answer with a lie.

"I do not know Grafton at all, so I could not tell you if there is anything wrong with the village. But I do wonder if there are any great families about your town. Anyone whom I would know by chance."

Julia stopped dancing and stepped out of line. He followed her. "Is there something the matter, Miss Woodville?" he asked.

She scoffed, unable to hold back her annoyance. "What if there isn't anyone lofty and titled living near Grafton? Does that change your opinion of my family and me? Are we less because we are not dukes and earls?" she asked him.

He glanced around, looking to see who was listening to their conversation. Julia did the same, but where he was embarrassed, she would never be. She had nothing to be ashamed of. Her family was well off and law-abiding. They may not be noble, but they were very respectable gentry, which was just as good.

"Of course not. I would never suggest such a thing, Miss Woodville," he replied, his eyes beseeching, yet she did not believe him. He had insinuated as much, and she knew she could never look to him as a potential suitor because of his opinions.

"Thank you for the dance, Mr. Watts. I wish you a pleasant evening." Julia dipped into a curtsy and walked away. She made it as far as the supper room doors before Lord Chilsten caught up to her.

"It did not look as if your dance with Mr. Watts went well, Julia." He pulled her to a stop, and she huffed out a breath, trying to calm her annoyance at Mr. Watts and men in general.

"Why is it that gentlemen such as yourselves can be so

snobbish? We were not brought up to be so, not with anyone, yet Mr. Watts made me feel like I was less of a person simply because I'm from Grafton and have no title."

"Grafton is a lovely little village. I often pass through there on my way to see Lord Billington."

She stared up at him, not having known that. "You've been through the village that I live nearby, my lord?"

"Yes." He nodded, seemingly proud of the fact, before throwing her a consoling look. "Do not think another minute on what Mr. Watts said. At least you now know he is not for you. We merely need to look for another."

"Who would you suggest?" she asked, glancing about the room. "I would like to find the love of my life before the end of the Season. Is it not bad form if a woman returns to town the following year and has to have a second Season? I shudder at the thought of those poor ladies who are on their third and fourth."

"Yes," he agreed with her. "That would be unfortunate for ladies indeed, and I have never thought it fair, considering there are bachelors in town who are five and thirty and are yet to marry."

"Which begs me to ask, how old are you, Lord Chilsten? Are you as ancient as that?"

He burst out laughing, his eyes twinkling in mirth. "No, I'm not as wise as that, but I am six and twenty. Much older than yourself."

"I'm one and twenty, and that is not much older, and women mature much quicker than men. Is that not true?" she asked him.

"Like a fine wine ripened with age and only grows sweeter by the year." He watched her, his eyes heavy-lidded, sparking with some thoughts he was yet to share with her. If he ever would.

She wondered what it was that flittered through his mind just then that made her stomach clench. "Your words always seem to have a second meaning, my lord. Do behave."

He grinned, but conceded. "Very well. I shall not tease you anymore, but back to finding you a love match." He looked out over the sea of heads. "What about Lord Spencer? He is reportedly ready for a wife and has no scandals attached to him." Lord Chilsten pointed him out, and Julia took in the man in question.

He, too, was blessed with fine looks and impeccable clothing and appearance, but he was very short for a man. Too short for her. "He would barely come up to my waist."

"Some women would say that was a perfect height," he drawled, throwing her a teasing glance.

She slapped his shoulder, unsure what he meant by such words and, right at this moment, not sure she wanted to hear. "You're incorrigible. You're supposed to be helping me and not suggesting men whom I would look absurd standing next to."

"So you need a man as tall as I am or near about?" he asked her.

"Of course, or only a fraction smaller."

"But what if you fall in love with a barely five-foot-nine gentleman?"

She sighed, not wanting to think of such things. She supposed she would have to marry him and ensure with any portraits done of them together she was sitting. But they would look an odd pair, and she had never wanted to glance down at her husband. She wanted to look up at him. And she did not want to look unfeminine beside him, a tall meg towering over him like an ogre.

At that moment, she met Chilsten's dark, stormy eyes

and lost herself. "You are a nice height. And if you remember our time alone, we fit together agreeably. I want something similar, and I do not think it is too much to ask."

He cleared his throat, pulling at his cravat. "That seems reasonable enough. I will ensure to only point you toward gentlemen who are not deficient in height."

"Thank you." She studied the throng, her eyes alighting on Lord Roberts. "What of Lord Robert's background? Do you know much about him?"

"Best to keep away from Roberts. He's rumored to have a mistress and a temper toward the fairer sex."

Julia gasped. "Surely you jest. He seems so very sweet. I mean..." she said, hoping the heat on her cheeks did not give her away at how inappropriate her words were to his answer. "He does not look like a man who would seek comfort in the arms of a whore or be violent."

Cyrus scoffed, shaking his head. "Surely it is you who jests, Miss Julia. You ought to know that men may still support a mistress elsewhere, no matter how much they may love their wives. It is as common as having tea at Gunter's."

A cold chill ran down her spine, having never thought that her husband would do such a thing. Certainly not if they were a love match. And what of her sisters? Did they have to suffer through the humiliation of their husbands, men she believed loved her sisters dearly? "Are you saying that my brothers-in-law may have lovers outside the marriage bed? That my sisters' health could be at risk due to their husbands' duplicitous ways?"

"No, of course not," he choked out. "I know that the duke and viscount do not have a mistress. Your sisters are well satisfied both in mind and heart. I only meant that some men, no matter what they may say to your face to please you, may still do something opposite to what you think they may do."

Julia studied Chilsten a moment, the question in her mind needing to be voiced. "Have you ever had a mistress?"

"I should not even answer such a question. You're an unmarried maid, and this is not an appropriate conversation," he said, doing his best to keep his eyes forward and not on her.

She persisted, needing to know, for some unknown reason. "Tell me. I'm not so young and innocent, as you well know." He stubbornly remained quiet, and she ground her teeth. "Tell me this then, at least. Will you seek one once you're married?"

He did look at her then, his eyes dipping to her lips. She fought the urge to bite her bottom lip at his inspection. "I should hope that my marriage is passionate enough that I will not seek comfort elsewhere."

"And that hope would extend to your wife," she added. Like any gentleman, no wife wanted a passionless marriage, surely. Still, if Lord Chilsten thought she would suffer such a fate, allow her husband to have a mistress when she could not seek a lover outside the bonds of marriage, he would be mistaken. In truth, she would not, but he did not know that, and she wanted it to remain that way.

"I would not allow you to have a lover if we were married, Miss Julia. You may be certain of that," he quipped.

The hair on the back of her neck rose. Whether from the mention of his marrying her, or his statement, she could not say, but nor could she allow him to believe such a thing. What is good for one sex is good for the other. "Then I would not allow you to have one either, should we marry. I would not suffer such humiliation."

"If I were married to you, I do not think I would need a whore to satisfy me. Not if our interlude last year was any indication. I do not believe," he added, leaning toward her and whispering to ensure privacy, "our marriage would be passionless. I think it would be the opposite."

Julia remembered to breathe, and she ignored the need that spiked through her. It was always the same. Whenever he mentioned their one kiss, her one demand on him last Season, always her body remembered and craved what it had experienced.

"It was so long ago, one hardly remembers," she lied.

"We cannot have that," he said, taking her hand and placing it on his arm before he casually strolled from the room as if they were about to take the air.

They walked past several couples idling in the foyer before slipping into the dining room. Cyrus closed the door, the sound of the lock loud and final.

"You cannot remember our kiss, Miss Woodville? I must not have been up to my usual wolfish self."

"There is no need to repeat the kiss, my lord. I was merely making a statement of truth. I was not asking for a repeat of our time together."

"I disagree," he said before stepping against her, his large, strong hand cupping her face. "Time for another lesson," he said, saving her from thinking of nothing but Chilsten and his wicked mouth on hers.

CHAPTER
FIVE

Cyrus inwardly swore at his antics. He was walking a tightrope that would topple him to his ruination and that of his child. He needed a wife of stature, and many were available in the *ton*—dowager duchesses and marchionesses, ready and willing to marry a rogue like him.

And yet here he was, in a dining room of all romantic places, kissing a virginal debutante for the second time. Julia melted into his arms, her lips as soft and supple as he remembered them. Their discussion on lovers outside the bonds of marriage had made him want her with a need that went beyond reasonable thought.

She was as distracting as any woman he had ever met, and the thought of her seeking a lover should she marry a boobie made him want to cry out at the shame of such a tragedy. Julia deserved passion, numerous kisses, and love. Her reaction to him told her she could not suffer a loveless marriage, and if he were to help her navigate the marriage mart, he would ensure she succeeded with one.

"You're so beautiful," he said, breaking the kiss and meeting her eyes.

She blinked at him, her lips glistening from their kiss. He could not deny himself. He kissed her again, pushing her against the wall. Their tongues tangled, her hands slipped beneath his waistcoat and his shirt. His, too, sought what they craved. He squeezed her small waist, reveling in the feel of her ass, before grasping one long, lithe thigh.

Hell, she had long legs. The thought of them wrapped about his waist made him rock hard.

She gasped as he lifted her leg against his hip, pushing against her, showing her what he wanted without words. Not that he could have her. She would never be his, but he could tease them both and show her what she should look for in a husband and lover.

Sin and delicious pleasure.

He was as wicked as they came, yet he could not stop himself. Could not halt the need to revel in what she made him feel, sink into this ecstasy between them and stay there as long as she would allow.

She pulled back, staring at him, her cheeks pinkened from their embrace, but her eyes held a question he knew she wanted to be answered.

"What are we doing? It is one thing for you to help guide me through the muddy waters of finding a husband within the *ton*, but it is quite another to kiss me in an abandoned room at a ball. Need I remind you that you're not seeking me for a bride, and I'll only marry a man who loves me? Kissing me is not helping my cause, my lord."

Cyrus felt himself gape. How had she been able to think when he was kissing her so? His mind was nothing but chaotic thoughts and needs. Was he more rattled by their kiss than she was? Mayhap it did not confound her at all?

The thought was a little mortifying for his rakish wiles.

He took a deep breath and set her leg back onto the floor, stepping away from her and giving her space. She remained leaning against the wall, her breasts straining against her bodice with each breath. No matter how calm and collected her voice may be, her body defied her words. She had been as affected by the kiss as he had, and the look in her brown eyes told him she would welcome another if he pressed his suit.

"You are right. This is not at all helpful, and if we're caught it will only make our lives difficult and cause scandal for our families. I do apologize, Julia. I shall not kiss you again. I will ensure that all our future meetings are public and above reproach," he said, hoping he could keep his promise.

The thought of his daughter being ridiculed because he could not find a wife high enough in society to protect her would never do. If only Julia were a dowager duchess or marchioness and agreed to marry him before she knew of his scandal, all would go swimmingly.

She nodded. "Good evening, my lord." Julia fled the room, her skirts rustling as she walked quickly across the foyer and back toward the ballroom. Cyrus shut the door, leaning his head against the dark oak. He needed to stop this madness. He would begin looking in earnest for a wife who suited his needs on the morrow. Assist Julia when she required clarification or assistance.

He would not slip again. She deserved better than he could ever give her, and he was determined to give it to her if he could not give her anything else.

. . .

J ulia strolled through Hyde Park the following afternoon, her sisters, the Duchess of Derby and Viscountess Leigh, beside her talking of tonight's event, a ball at Lady Owens's estate on the outskirts of Mayfair. The ball was a mask, and the invitations had been limited and most sought after. Julia wasn't fool enough to know that she had been invited merely because her sisters were now part of the upper echelon of society in London.

She held her parasol above her head and absently listened to her sisters discuss transport and what gowns they intended to wear. She heard snippets of information regarding her own dress, but her mind was not on the ball. It was occupied elsewhere.

In particular, on Lord Chilsten, who sat in a boat on the Serpentine with the Dowager Duchess of Barker lounging before him like some Roman goddess just waiting for him to feed her grapes.

She felt her mouth gape, and her brow wrinkle as she watched Chilsten plop the green fruit into Her Grace's willing mouth before they laughed at their antics.

She schooled her features before her sisters noticed her reaction to his lordship's seductive ploys on the water toward his new lover. She had little doubt that was what the woman was to the man. He was a rogue, after all, one of London's worst, and she knew better than anyone how well he played that part, how his kisses stole a woman's common sense and made her want things that would never be.

He had told her as much himself. He required a wife of status. To see him floating about the lake with the Dowager Duchess of Barker said without words the time was now and he had made his choice.

Not that she could hate him for his choice. He had never lied to her. Her own foolish heart had allowed her to hope after two breathless, devastating kisses that there might be more between them than she first thought.

She tore her gaze away just as the touch of Hailey's hand on her arm brought her to a halt.

"Julia, you're a million miles away. We've been asking you what you find so interesting on the lake, but then we see who may have interested you, which now interests us," Hailey said, grinning.

Julia looked past her elder sister to Isla, who had a knowing grin on her pretty face too. "Do you like Lord Chilsten? I have met him several times since he's good friends with my husband and Hailey's. He would be a good match for you," she finished, twirling her parasol for good measure.

"A shame about his wife, although very little is known about her," Hailey stated, watching Lord Chilsten with contemplation.

"He does not say much at all about his wife. All I know is that she passed away not long after their marriage," Julia mentioned, trying to keep her attention off the man in discussion.

"It is odd that he returned to town to enjoy the Season when he is not officially out of mourning, do you not agree?" Isla said. "But then, he does have a reputation for skirting the rules of society. I suppose it should not shock us all that much."

Julia nodded, frowning in thought. "Gentlemen of his stature, I suppose, do not see the need to obey the rules."

"Nothing more scandalous and enough to get the *ton's* tongues waggling than feeding the Dowager Duchess of Barker on the Serpentine." Hailey nodded toward Lady

Shaw, who stood at the shore of the lake watching the marquess and his latest conquest float about as if they were the only two people in the park. "Lady Shaw looks ready to huff out fire at their antics. I should hate to think what she would do should they kiss."

A cold shiver ran down Julia's spine, and her attention snapped back to the pair. "You jest. Lord Chilsten would not dare do such a scandalous thing," she said, hoping that was true. The thought of him kissing another woman after their shared kiss the evening before left her all at sea.

"I have heard he has done worse than that," Hailey said before shrugging. "I should not mention any more. You're not married yet, and this conversation, if it stays on Lord Chilsten, will not remain appropriate."

What more did her sister know that she did not? She glanced back at the lake, and her eyes locked with Lord Chilsten's. He watched her from the boat, and although she could hear the tinkling laugh of the dowager duchess, she knew he was not listening.

Julia could feel his eyes upon her person as if they were once again alone in the dining room, his hands clutching her body, shifting her against him and making her crave things she should not. Not until she was a married woman, in any case.

The dowager duchess said something, pulling Lord Chilsten's attention from her. Was this the woman he would make his wife? Her Grace was one of the wealthiest widows in London and one of the youngest. They would suit each other well.

"The dowager duchess has a son, does she not?" Julia asked.

"Yes," Hailey said. "He is eight, I believe, and attends

Eton. The duchess does not need to marry if she does not wish to. Her son secures her position in society."

And she would be the lofty, powerful match that Lord Chilsten wanted. Had he kissed her last evening and then sought the comforting arms of the duchess later that night? Was he seducing her, while courting the dowager duchess? A lump formed in her throat, and she swallowed. Hard. This would never do. He was her friend. He was to help her find a husband who would fall in love with her and make her feel all the wonderful things she felt when she was in Lord Chilsten's arms.

She did not need to become some jealous, slighted debutante who had acted less than respectable with a man and was now paying the price for such inappropriate actions. If she felt jealous, it was her fault for allowing herself to hope for more than his lordship offered her.

Silly little innocent fool that she was.

CHAPTER
SIX

"Miss Woodville, how very opportune it is for us to meet. I saw you across the park and had to come to speak to you."

Julia pulled her gaze from Lord Chilsten to Lord Perry, forcing herself to forget her wayward troubles and concentrate on a man who may become of interest to her. "Lord Perry, it is lovely to see you," she said, dipping into a curtsy. "Are you taking the air with your sister, or do we find you all alone this afternoon?" she asked, glancing past him and not seeing Lady Sally, whom he often escorted on outings.

"Just me this afternoon, but I hope that is to your liking." He gestured toward the path. "Shall we take a walk?" he asked, smiling at her sisters, who stood listening like a pair of seasoned matrons, which they were anything but.

"That would be lovely," she answered, taking his offered arm.

"We shall accompany you but walk a little behind," her sister Hailey stated, throwing them both a warm smile.

They strolled along the path, other couples and the *ton*

doing the same. However, like Lord Chilsten, some boated on the lake while others picnicked on the lawns. "It is a lovely day today, is it not?" she said, fighting to think of conversational ideas. She was dreadful at trying to see if she had any connections with other gentlemen if she could not find something of interest.

"I find you lovely," he answered. "Does that count?" he asked, his grin making her cheeks heat.

She chuckled, unsure how to answer such a bold statement. Lord Perry appeared to have more gumption than she first thought, and she did enjoy a nice compliment when given. What lady would not? "Thank you." She smiled, unable to wipe the grin from her lips. "I must say, however, my lord, that no matter your flattery, you have yet to call on me. Is there a reason as to why you have not?"

His gaze flicked to the lake, and she refused to look to where she knew Lord Chilsten floated about with the widowed duchess. "I did not think my presence would be welcome, but seeing you today...well, you may be assured that I shall call on you and often after today."

Julia knew what he was referring to. She and Lord Chilsten were often seen together, and mayhap that had been hindering her ability to find a husband instead of helping as she hoped. Not that Lord Perry would have to worry about her being any longer occupied with the marquess. Their arrangement was well and truly over after today. He looked more than happy with the dowager duchess, and she would not make a fool of herself pining for a man who wished to remain a rake and make a beast with two backs all over London with any willing lady.

"I look forward to your company," she said. "Are you attending the mask this evening at Lady Owens's? It's the event of the Season, it is said."

"I will be in attendance. May I ask if you'll be easy to recognize? I should hate to spend the night searching for you only to leave disappointed when I cannot locate you, Miss Woodville."

He stared down at her, and she could see in his eyes that he was in earnest. That he fully intended to seek her out and court her, perhaps? Her stomach twisted into a ball of nerves, and hope took flight. Was Lord Perry the man she had been waiting for? No one else had made her feel as giddy as he had just done. Well, at least no one but Lord Chilsten, but he was not an option, and she needed to remember that fact.

"If I tell you what I'm wearing or what mask I shall have on, that will give you an unfair advantage. You ought to recognize me no matter what I wear or how I present myself," she teased, wanting to see if he could follow suit. She could never fall in love with a man who did not know how to flirt or be a little wild of heart.

"Oh, I shall recognize you, Miss Woodville, no matter your costume, but it would only make me find you faster should I know the particulars."

For the first time this Season, Julia found herself smiling and interested in more than superficial discussions that she'd had so many times before with the other gentlemen who had paid court or danced with her.

Lord Perry seemed well versed in the art of teasing, and she liked that about him. He was as refreshing as the day was at the park. They walked along, greeting others who passed them as they went.

"May I ask that I have the first dance then if you will not disclose what you're to wear? I insist, Miss Woodville."

Julia could see no harm in such a request, and she wanted to dance with him, something she was yet to do. So far, his company had been enjoyable, and something told her that dancing and being in his lordship's arms would be just the same. "If you like," she answered.

"I would like it very much, and I hope you would too. Or is that a little too bold of me?"

"Perhaps a very little," she stated. "But all the same, I shall save a place for you on my card." She glanced behind her, startled to see her sister's eyes alight with expectation and delight. Julia turned back to Lord Perry and tried to ignore the hope her siblings were taking from this sojourn in the park.

"You have a country estate in Kent, I believe. Is that so, or have I made a mistake with that observation?"

"No mistake," he said, a small, satisfied smile crossing his face. "Allenvale House is where I spend most of my time. I understand you're from Grafton in Northamptonshire. That is a long way from my home. It is no wonder our paths have not crossed until now."

"It is very understandable, is it not?"

"Would you settle far from your parents and where you grew up, Miss Woodville?"

She had never thought about it until now, but then she supposed all of her unmarried sisters would have to face such a prospect in time. Unless the gentlemen they married lived near Grafton, of course. "As much as I will miss my family, I know that I will settle elsewhere, but having a family of my own soon soothes any ache of sadness that thought incurs."

"I should think any man who becomes privileged to be your husband will do all they can to make you happy and content."

His lordship stared at her, and her mind blanked, unable to form any witty reply to lighten the moment.

"How very true, Lord Perry," Lord Chilsten stated, the dowager duchess on his arm and watching her with interest.

Julia swallowed, having not seen Chilsten climb out of the boat or make his way toward them.

"I should hope any gentleman who courts a lady in town this Season or following would always strive for such outcomes." He turned to the duchess, raising his brow. "Do you not agree, Your Grace?"

"Of course," she said, in a sultry voice that lifted the hackles on Julia's neck. "I've been fortunate already to have married for love and affection. I do hope you do too, Miss Woodville," she said mockingly. "That is your name, is it not? *Miss* Julia Woodville?"

Was the widowed duchess mocking her for her common name? Julia glanced at Chilsten and noted he seemed not aware of how the duchess had twisted her name to make a point with it. "Were you not Miss Parker prior to marrying the duke? I must offer my condolences, Your Grace. You must still be very heartbroken by his loss," Lord Perry said, coming to Julia's defense.

Her Grace's eyes narrowed, and Julia felt the muscle of Lord Perry's arm tighten under her hand. She schooled her features, not knowing that the duchess was of a similar birthright to her own. Lord Perry was a champion defending the slight to her person and her family.

"It has been very hard," Her Grace agreed, glancing up at Chilsten with a pout. The woman was a wonderful actress, but she wasn't fooling Julia. She could read straight through the woman's falseness, and she understood only too well that she was looking at Lord Chilsten to be her next lover or husband.

The thought made Julia's skin crawl, and she fought to

control her ire. Her annoyance at both the forward duchess and Chilsten for allowing such a woman to cling to him as if he were some savior she could not live without.

He was just a man like any other.

He is not.

She glanced about the park, anywhere but the two people before her, wanting this conversation to end. She may be Lord Chilsten's friend, but that did not mean she wanted his potential wives and lovers pushed before her, flaunted, and declared as if she would not mind.

You should not mind.

Julia swallowed. But she did. Deep down, she had hoped he would see her as the woman who would suit him most.

Bile rose in her throat. She hated the thought of the two of them being married.

Enough, her mind screamed. *Leave. Now. Before you're privy to any more of his doings that you have no right to be jealous of. Take Lord Perry and walk away. Try to find what you feel when around Chilsten with someone else. Try harder if it is not happening naturally.*

"Well, we must be going. I see my sisters are gesturing for us to rejoin them," Julia lied, pulling Lord Perry away from Chilsten and his latest quarry.

Chilsten glanced over his shoulder and located her siblings. "They appear engrossed in their conversation with Lady Shaw." He turned to her, grinning in that mischievous way that made her want to swoon at his feet. "But if you wish to depart, good day to you both. I'm certain we shall meet again. This evening perhaps. At the masked ball," he said.

Julia nodded, wanting to get as far away from Chilsten and how he made her feel. Jealous, angry, wanton, sad, and happy. Too many emotions to count. "Maybe we shall. Good day to you both."

Julia sighed her relief when Lord Perry followed her without another word. They walked toward her sisters in silence, her mind too full of Chilsten to think of anything else to say to the man at her side.

A good match for her and a man who seemed to evoke some emotion from her, similar to Chilsten. Could she make that sentiment grow? Could she build on that small spark and make it into an inferno that her body craved as much as air?

As much as she craved Chilsten?

She hoped it would be so. Chilsten seemed determined to marry well and so too would she. Her family expected so much of her now that her sisters were part of the *ton*. She could not let them down.

Julia smiled up at Lord Perry. "This evening, maybe we could supper together too, my lord? You are more than welcome to join my sisters and me, the duchess and viscountess if you like."

Lord Perry nodded, his eyes alight with pleasure. "That would be most welcome, Miss Julia. I shall count down the hours."

And she would too, but not for the same reason. Her reason stood several feet behind her. Chilsten's gaze made the hairs on the back of her neck prickle just as he made her blood pump fast and her lungs breathless.

Damn the rogues and rakes of London. They ought to be outlawed.

CHAPTER
SEVEN

Cyrus was not sure what he had done to make Julia flee him in the park this afternoon, but he could take a guess. He adjusted his mask, slumped against a wall, and watched as the lady herself laughed and talked with several friends at the ball.

Of course, she was utterly charming and captivated all who spoke with her. Himself included. He was not immune to her charms, knowing what she felt like in his embrace. Perfection indeed.

Not that he should be thinking of such things. Right now, he could have the Dowager Duchess of Barker hidden away at his London home and doing all and everything the rogue in him craved. But not anymore.

This afternoon the moment he had spied Julia watching him, the devastation that had crossed her visage had told him that she felt far more for him than she led him to believe.

Friends indeed.

Could such a thing even be possible between a man and woman? Especially if that man and woman could not keep their hands from each other whenever they were alone, no matter what they declared outwardly?

He had told her the complications in his life required him to marry a woman of status. His last marriage had only taken place so his child would be legitimate. He knew his next bride needed to be high born within the *ton*, not merely related to some who were. The dowager duchess fit the position perfectly.

But she was not whom he wanted.

Julia wore more rouge on her lips this evening than he had ever seen before, and with the black mask covering her eyes and nose, her wickedly long lashes made her appear foreign and mysterious.

He downed the last of his brandy, placed the crystal tumbler on the nearby mantel, and debated what to do.

For his child's sake, he ought to leave her alone. Let her be courted by Lord Perry, whom she seemed to like well enough today at the park. He clamped his jaw, spotting the fellow not too far from Julia.

The first notes of the ball's opening dance sounded in the room, and a flurry of couples took to the floor. Julia seemed to look for Lord Perry, who was already at her side before she could turn her head.

Was she setting her cap on him? A lump of dread settled in his gut. He did not like the notion.

"I've seen that look before, and should I be a betting man, I'd lay blunt down that I know your next move."

The laughing tones of his good friend, the Duke of Derby, sounded beside him, pulling Cyrus from his obsession with Julia Woodville dancing with Lord Perry and looking far too happy about that fact.

"Am I that obvious?" he sighed, running a hand over his jaw. The stubble prickled his palm. He really ought to have shaved before leaving this evening. "I thought I was better at hiding my thoughts and deliberations. Obviously, I am not."

"Not when it comes to my sister-in-law, Julia." The duke clapped him on the shoulder, laughing. "Come, man, what are you thinking, truly? I have seen you together several times. Is there something that you need to admit to? Maybe even to yourself?"

Cyrus wanted to admit all his sins to his friend. Have Derby tell him that Julia would not mind his indiscretion with the maid that resulted in a child, but he was fooling himself to hear such words. Derby and Julia would be disappointed, and Julia would never marry him. How crass to sleep with one's servant and have a child as a result. She would want a marriage to a man who came with no scandalous history.

He was not that man. Not even before he had slept with his maid.

"We are friends, and that is all. I do like her, but it is nothing more than that." He paused, trying to locate her on the dance floor. "I said I would assist her in choosing a husband who is right for her. One who is not sullied by debt or is a rogue who will break her heart."

"So with those points, I assume you have ruled yourself out of contention?" Derby stated.

"Of course," he agreed. "I'm far too sullied—and wish to remain so—to marry such an innocent miss."

"Marry again, you mean," Derby said, watching him. "You have not stated who your wife was. I'm sorry to hear of her passing. Was she from a family I would know in Scotland?"

Cyrus hated these types of conversations. He was a wretch for sleeping with Fanny, even though the lass chased him long before he tupped her. She had not been a virgin, and he knew she had been with others, yet he had gotten her with child. English marquess and Scottish duke or not, he would never falter in his responsibilities like his own father. He had traveled to Scotland the moment he heard she was weeks from giving birth.

Even if that meant he had left but a day after his devastating kiss with Julia. One that he had not expected. A kiss that had made him want things for the first time, challenged his mindset to remain a rogue forever.

If only things were different...

"Her name was Fanny, and no, she was not from any prominent family." He cleared his throat, not wanting to admit his shame at having tupped his servant. He shook his head, wondering what he had been thinking of at the time. Or, more truthfully, what his base needs had wanted without thought at all.

"Lord Perry would be a good match for Miss Julia. I will discuss him further this evening with her. But please do not take my interest in the miss any further than that. I am her friend as much as I am yours, and nothing untoward is happening between us." Or would happen again, he amended.

The duke narrowed his eyes but seemed to accept his words. "Very well then. Your words will ease my wife's worries, and you know I never like to see my wife displeased. Do not do anything that would cause Julia harm, Chilsten. You are my friend, and I do not want to have a falling out with you."

Cyrus nodded, ceding the duke's point. "I understand, and you can be assured I will not overstep my bounds and ruin her chances of a good match. I am there only to help her. Nothing more."

"Good man," Derby said before leaving him to his musings. He spied Julia dancing yet again, but not with Lord Perry. This time Mr. Watts jostled her about on the ballroom floor. Both of them laughed and smiled during the quick and lively dance.

How beautiful she was, animated with joy.

The words she had stated to Derby haunted him, mocking him. He needed to keep their conversations and rendezvous public without the threat of scandal. But how was he to do what he promised, for whenever he was around her, he wanted to scurry her away and have her in every way he could.

She would run for the hills if she knew what he wanted to do with her. Where he wanted to kiss her, taste her. He took a calming breath. Where he would have her.

God damn it all to hell. He was doomed, and he needed to stop before he doomed her along with him.

The night was magical, the ballroom filled with opulent gowns and masks that gave the night an air of mystery. Of course, she had not been able to recognize some people until they spoke in conversation, but others she could pick out in an instant.

Lord Chilsten one of them.

All evening he had not moved from his location. He remained beside the mantel, quiet and watchful of the *ton* as they danced and drank and ate.

Supper had been enjoyable, and she had spoken further with Lord Perry, whom she was certain was courting her in truth. A positive turn for her in a Season that had been otherwise a little disappointing regarding gentlemen admirers. Thankfully Lord Payne had stopped pressing his suit when she started to show interest in others. Not that he had ever made a formal declaration of love toward her.

Julia stood with her sisters and their husbands as they discussed the ball and gossip that circulated about London this week. She often included herself with a *yes*, or *no*, or *oh really*, but nothing further than that, for she could not stop watching Lord Chilsten and the Dowager Duchess of Barker, who had found him at last and would not leave his side.

Not that the man seemed disappointed by that fact.

The rogue.

She had wanted to speak to him herself. He was supposed to be helping her, but he seemed a little cool and aloof. Normally he would have sought her out, spoken to her of the few gentlemen she had already danced with, but tonight he had not.

He had kept his distance and had barely glanced at her. Well, of that she was not entirely certain. She could only assume so because he had been engaged in conversation with someone else every time she looked at him.

She pondered all this, surreptitiously watching him still and hoping no one noticed. Unlikely tonight, since everyone wore masks, and her sister Hailey had her maid paint her eyes with a dark coal-like shade that made her look even more secretive beneath her mask.

Her sisters took to the dance floor, leaving her for a moment alone, and she tried to blend further into the throng of guests, no longer wanting to dance or be distracted by anyone. She merely wished to be alone, to watch Chilsten and see what he was up to. Not that she had any claim on him, she did not. He may do whatever he wished, but still, something within her rejected the idea of that. She wanted to be alone with him and no one else. She wanted to kiss his sweet lips and feel his hands upon her person.

She wanted him...

The Duchess Barker looked in her direction, and the smugness on her pinched visage made her blood run cold. The woman wanted Chilsten too, and from the looks of it, she was succeeding in gaining what she wanted.

Anger thrummed within her, and Julia fought not to glare at them both. What was he playing at, kissing her and others, such as Her Grace? Did he think that his lack of control excused the kisses he'd bestowed on her because he had told her she did not meet his expectations for a wife?

She should not be so annoyed, she had kissed him back, knowing this truth, but her heart would not abide by sensible thought. She was incensed, he had played her for the naïve, innocent fool she was, and she would not stand for it.

"Julia, here you are. I have found you at last." Her friend, Reign, bussed her cheek before standing beside her. "I'm late. I apologize. I was waylaid."

"That is no problem," she said, glad that her friend was there finally before she did something stupid like stomp across the room and scratch the haughty duchess's piercing blue eyes out.

Reign studied her a moment before her gaze flicked to Lord Chilsten. Her lips thinned into a displeased line. "I see Lord Chilsten has moved on to greener pastures, ones willing to feed his endless appetite."

Julia bit down her laugh. Reign always had a way with words, innocent enough but cutting in truth. "It does seem to be the case. I saw them earlier today at the park. They were boating together. I can only assume he's found his new marchioness," Julia stated, hoping she sounded matter-of-fact and not as devastated as she was in truth. Her foolish, innocent heart had so much to learn when it came to rakes of the *ton*.

"I know he requires a wife of status, but we've kissed. I thought..." She shrugged, swallowing the lump that rose in her throat. "I thought that it may mean something that he had kissed me. That mayhap he had changed his mind. How foolish I've acted."

Reign threw her a consoling look. "Maybe a little, but kisses from rogues are hard to deny oneself."

Julia studied her friend a moment, wondering if she had truths to disclose. She waited, but when Reign did not elaborate, she did not press. Her friend would tell her anything she wanted her to know when she was ready.

"Do you think they're lovers already?" Julia asked, the words thick and difficult to say out loud.

"The duchess is draped over him like a bedsheet. I think it is safe to say that they are." Reign turned to her. "I'm so sorry, dearest. But at least you can be sure he will not disclose the indiscretion between you. He would not dare with Derby being your brother-in-law and his friend."

All true, and some comfort, she supposed. He had not told anyone of their first kiss last Season before he scuttled off to Scotland, so he seemed to want to keep what happened between them a secret.

"I'm going to go out to the terrace for some air. Do you wish to join me?" Julia asked.

Reign shook her head. "I cannot, not yet at least. I promised the next dance to Lord Lupton-Gage."

Julia raised her brow, having not known Reign knew the marquess so well. She smiled, hoping her friend too would find a match worthy of her love. "Very well. I shall not be long. I will come to find you after your dance."

"I look forward to it."

Julia made her way through the crowd, taking a sigh of relief as the outdoor, cooling air revitalized her. The room was a crush, and movement was almost impossible other than on the dance floor. She strolled to the railing, looking out over the gardens. Many people were outdoors. Groups of friends sat at several tables, all illuminated with candles, an extension of sorts to the ballroom on this balmy evening.

"Miss Julia, I thought you may like a glass of ratafia," Lord Perry suggested, handing her a glass.

She smiled, studying his lordship, needing to make herself see others for who they were and not what they were lacking compared to Lord Chilsten. His lordship was lost to her, the dowager duchess would become the next Marchioness of Chilsten and there was little she could do about that fact.

Whereas Lord Perry was more than willing to settle down and start a family. Julia smiled, taking the glass he held out for her and taking a sip. "Thank you, my lord. You're very kind to bring me a cooling repast."

"My pleasure." His lordship's eyes darkened with heat, and Julia knew she could love this man in time. He seemed to know how to flirt and be a little mischievous. Not as devilish as Chilsten, but that was no failing. Julia inwardly cringed, stopping herself from going down that path of thought. Lord Chilsten's road led to a dead-end, and no longer was she willing to walk it.

"Shall we stroll?" she asked him.

"I would like that." They moved along the terrace, farther from the other guests to where the shadow of the great house hid them a little from view. "I had hoped we could talk in private. I wanted to say how very glad I am that I've met you, and I hope we may continue our friend-ship with more interludes such as this."

His words made her feel warm and comfortable, like she had been wrapped up into a fur coat and held within strong arms. "I would like that as well, my lord," she agreed.

Without warning, he reached out, placing a curl of hair behind her ear. "Would it be bold of me to ask that you save each ball's first and last dance we attend for me?"

Julia stared up at Lord Perry. Was he saying such a lovely thing? She supposed in truth that he was courting her, and an offer would soon be forthcoming should they continue to get along well.

Did she want him to propose? Could she see herself married to the man before her for the rest of her life?

The image of Lord Chilsten flashed before her, taunting her, and she pushed it away, locked it down so it could not confuse her anymore.

"I would like nothing more, my lord," she answered, hoping the disappointment that stabbed at her with her answer was merely nerves and nothing more sinister.

Like unrequited love for another.

EIGHT

"I would suggest you let go of Miss Woodville's hair this very instant and move back, Perry," the warning voice of Lord Chilsten sounded behind her.

Julia turned, not having heard him approach them, and from the startled look upon Lord Perry's visage, he had not seen him either. Was the man lurking about? And why should he stalk at all, especially when he was so busy with the dowager duchess?

"I beg your pardon, Chilsten, but there is nothing to be so put out by. I was doing Miss Woodville a favor, not a disfavor, by repairing her hair."

Julia nodded, rounding on Chilsten. Her heart lurched with the burning anger that swirled in his eyes. Eyes that were pinned on Lord Perry with deadly intent.

"We are merely talking, my lord, just as everyone else is on the terrace, as you can see," she said, gesturing to the others who sat and strolled the area. "Do not make a scene."

"In the shadows, they are not," he stated, his attention moving to her for the first time. Disappointment clouded his eyes before he blinked, and it was gone. "If you would return to the ball, Lord Perry. I wish to have a word with Miss Woodville."

"You are not my guardian," she reminded him.

"No, but I am one of his closest friends, and I believe I have the right to speak to you about your conduct."

She gasped—the audacity of the man.

"I shall return to the ball and meet with you for the last dance, Miss Woodville, as planned."

Julia watched as Lord Perry disappeared through the terrace doors before she glared at Chilsten. "How dare you chastise me as if you have some right to do so. Friend of Derby's or not, you do not have any say in whom I speak to or dance with or whom I allow to touch me."

"He will not touch you again."

She scoffed, laughing at his highhandedness. "And you're going to stop him? I thought we agreed that I would find a gentleman who made my heart beat fast, and you would tell me if he were suitable in both respectabilities and financially. That he would have no hidden skeletons that would come back and ruin me in society later. Is that not correct?"

"That may be correct," he said, running a hand through his hair and leaving it on end. Julia swallowed a moan at how handsome the action made him appear. How bedraggled and similar to how he had looked after their first kiss a year ago. "But I no longer believe you should be touching or kissing any of the men who make your heart beat fast. It is not proper, and you'll be ruined."

"You're absurd," she said. "So it is alright for me to kiss

you, but no one else. Not that I would go about the *ton* kissing gentlemen to test them against my feelings, but who are you to say I cannot? If I want to kiss Lord Perry, I shall, and there is nothing you can do about it."

He growled, glaring at her, and the breath in her lungs hitched. "Do not try me, Julia. I will not want to hear that you've thrown yourself into Lord Perry's arms."

She raised her brow, not willing to be told what to do by a man who had no right to do so. "What do you think you will do to me should I go against your rule? Punish me in some way? Do not think my family will stand for that."

"Nor would they stand for you kissing men all about London like some harlot."

Julia felt her mouth gape, and she clenched her hands into fists, lest she slap him for his words. "Why cannot women be more like you're accusing me of? You've acted like a male harlot most of your adult life. Why should you be allowed to do what I cannot?"

"I am not a harlot," he argued.

She shrugged, stepping away from him and striding farther into the darkness. She did not know where she was going. She did not care, so long as it wasn't near his presence. "I speak as I find, and I find you are a male harlot."

He caught up to her, his strong hand circling her upper arm and dragging her to a halt. She looked past him and realized they had moved far from the others on the terrace. "If you say such a thing to me again, I shall put you over my knee and prove how much of a debauched male I can be."

Instead of causing fear to course through her veins, warmth and wonder rippled in its place. What did he mean by such words? She wanted to push him to his brink and find out how mad and wild the rogue could be.

She stared up at him and knew he was waiting for her.

Waiting to see if she had the nerve to stand up to him in this way. Something within her told her that she would forever be under his spell if she did not stand up to him now. Unable to defend herself when needed. To have a voice.

"Harlot," she repeated, unable to stop the smirk on her lips. "There, I said it. Now, what are you going to do about it?"

C yrus stared down at the hellion from Grafton and wondered when and how a woman who grew up in the country and was cossetted most of her life could speak to a man in such a way. Forward and opinionated and damn well brave. He wanted to chastise her, rebuke what she called him. But in truth, she was right. He had a terrible reputation, and it had left him in many scandals in the past. His marriage to his maid notwithstanding. Not that Julia knew of that shame, but one day she would, and he would again be found wanting by the chit before him.

He took her hand, found the first door leading into the house, and pulled her inside. The room was dark, closed for the ball, and perfect for his chastisement of her. Not that she would welcome such a discussion. Her mocking glance and lifted chin told him she was ready to laugh at him, mock him.

He wouldn't, *couldn't* have that.

"I warned you that I would put you over my knee if you called me a harlot one more time."

She laughed, walking over to a nearby settee and running her hand along the silk cushioning. "You wouldn't dare," she taunted, pinning him with her large brown eyes.

He stared back, need and determination thrumming

73

through him. He should turn and leave. He knew she was pushing him, testing him, and he was about to fail. Miserably. She chuckled, and it was the final straw.

He stormed up to her, bent, and hooked her over his shoulder. She gasped, her fisted hands pummeling his back.

"Put me down, you oaf. How dare you accost me simply because I have an opinion of you, which I might add, is completely accurate."

He slipped her off his shoulder, laying her on his lap when he sat, and holding her there. "I warned you, Julia. Now you must pay the price for your rudeness."

"My rudeness," she gasped as he slid her gown slowly up her legs. His cock hardened at the sight of her silk stockings and the pretty little blue-ribbon ties at her thighs. He could feel her rapid breath, but she didn't fight to get away, and that in itself was telling.

He took the opportunity to feel her thigh, warm and soft beneath his palm. Damn, he wanted her. "Do you have any idea what I want to do to you right now, Julia?" he asked.

She shook her head but did not answer. He glanced down at her and saw that she was biting her lip, her eyes closed.

"Well, I'm going to tell you...." His hand slipped farther along her thigh, the warmth between her legs teasing and intoxicating. "I want to slip my hand between your legs, touch you where no man has ever touched before. I want to caress you until you shatter in my lap, screaming my name."

She made a little mewling sound, shimmying on his lap, putting his hand wickedly close to doing what he threatened. He lifted her gown over her bottom, her muslin shift giving little discretion. "I warned you, did I not, that I would spank you if you called me a harlot."

"Yes, you warned me," she gasped as his hand squeezed one delicious ass cheek.

The crack of his hand coming down on her sweet ass sounded in the room. She moaned, her hands flexing into the cushions of the chair. "You spanked me," she gasped, looking at him for the first time. "How is it that it does not feel like a punishment?"

Hunger ripped through him, and he smacked her ass a second time. Her eyes grew heavy with desire, and he knew she was as lascivious as he was. He also knew she had little to no idea what that feeling meant or how to ease that sensation.

"You push me too far, Julia. Around you, I do not want to act the gentleman."

She squirmed off his lap to kneel at his side. Her hands came around him as she straddled his lap, pushing him to lean back on the settee. "What if I never feel whatever I'm feeling right now with anyone else whom I meet? Show me what I can have before duty takes me away from you."

Her words tore pain through his chest. He didn't want her to be ripped from him, and he certainly didn't want her to be as intimate as they had been so far with anyone else. Not even her bastard husband, whomever that faceless foe would eventually become.

He pulled her close, her body teasing his, her cunny pressed up against his cock, which ached in his breeches. "I should not touch you. I should never have brought you in here at all."

"But you did," she argued, boldly stealing a quick, soft kiss. "And now you must give me what I want. What we both want."

Oh, he wanted her. Of that, there was no doubt, but he would not take her. She deserved far better than a quick tup in a vacant room at a ball. But he could give her relief. He slipped his hand about her waist, delving beneath her gown. Her eyes sparkled like diamonds in the dark, her breathing fast as his hand grazed her mons, teasing her sweet lips.

She moaned, lifting herself a little on his lap and giving him more room to explore. He teased and rolled the sweet little beaded button under his fingers that he knew wanted to be petted. She undulated on his hand. Fire coursed through him, threatening to consume him whole.

"Tell me what you want," she gasped as his hand teased her opening, wet and dripping with the need for him.

"I want," he managed, swallowing a groan as she lowered herself a little on his hand, impaling herself on his finger. "I want to fuck you. I want my cock to be where my hand is right now. I want to guide you onto my dick and fuck you until you scream my name. That is what I want."

She moaned, kissing him, her tongue tangling with his. He was losing control. He could feel it. He ached, his balls tight and painful in his silk breeches. He wanted her to touch him, and he couldn't hold the plea from his voice when he asked.

"Touch me, Julia. For pity's sake, touch me before I die," he begged her.

She fumbled with his falls, his cock, hard and long, slipped into her hand when she released him from his bonds. He leaned against the settee and watched under hooded lids as she studied him. Her finger ran down the length of him, her thumb slipping across the top of his cock, wiping the bead of cum sitting there.

She slipped her thumb into her mouth, tasting him, and

he gaped. That, he had not expected. Was she trying to kill him in truth? "You undo me," he admitted.

A self-satisfied grin lifted her lips before she stroked him. Her hand tightened about his cock, making his wits spiral. They were on dangerous ground. Both of them touching each other as they knew was not proper. If they were caught, marriage would be the least of his problems. He knew his friends, now Julia's family, would want to kill him.

Even so, he could not stop. He could not halt savoring her in his arms. He pushed another finger into her wet heat, fucking her in a rhythm she enjoyed.

"Oh yes, Chilsten," she moaned, moving upon him.

"Cyrus. Not Chilsten." She stroked him with the same intoxicating madness that he did her. They became in sync, and for the first time in his life, having sex with the woman in his arms slipped from his mind. This was enough. Bringing each other to climax was almost more intimate than the act itself.

He pulled her lips to his with his free hand, kissing her with a force that left him reeling. Never had he felt like this with a woman, and he knew to see Julia married to anyone else would be the end of him.

His balls tightened further, and he pumped into her hand just as her pace increased, and he felt the first tremors of her release around his fingers. He kept his rhythm, wanting her to shatter as his release came forth. He pumped his seed over his shirt and waistcoat and knew the ball was over for him now. Not that it mattered, he had made her come, she had found pleasure in his arms, and he could not wait to do it again. Maybe even something a little naughtier next time.

"Cyrus," she cried his name just as he longed to hear.

She clutched at his shoulders as the last of her orgasm dissipated.

He stared at her, drinking in the vision of a woman well-satisfied. And not just any woman, but the one who disassembled him in every way and maddened him too, in truth.

She slumped against him, her lips making small, nibbling kisses against his neck. "This is what you feel every time you're with a woman? And women can feel the same as men?" she asked him, wonder in her voice.

"Yes, a good lover, male or female, can make their partner feel as we do now. Of course, should I fuck you, well, that is another type of orgasm, but just as satisfying."

"Well," she breathed, looking up to meet his eye. "I would not have known that the body was so wickedly good. I had no notion at all this was possible between a couple."

He grinned, dipping his head to steal another kiss from her. "Such conversation with your parents may be awkward, but now you know the truth."

"Yes, now I know what I want," she whispered, her hand playing with his chest. "You made me feel so wonderful. How will I ever turn my attention to another when I know what you can do to me."

He groaned, the truth of her words hitting him as if someone had punched his gut. The knowledge haunted him, and he understood that watching her walk from him and marry another would be torturous.

But he was a rogue. A man who did not know how to be loyal, not for long periods of time. What if another woman crossed his path and he wanted her as much as he wanted Julia? He would break Julia's heart, and he could not live with such guilt. Better to let her marry someone else worthy, a man who did not sleep with his servants and get them with child. She would hate him if she married him only to find out the truth.

Maybe she would not. *Give her a choice and see,* a voice whispered in his mind. He dismissed it, not willing to give himself any hope. He deserved none.

CHAPTER
NINE

J ulia ordered her horse early the following morning, needing to ride, feel the wind in her face, and think. That above anything else.

The previous night in Cyrus's arms had left her flailing and unsure of what she should do. She knew for certain that no matter who she had met so far, none of them brought forth in her the feelings that overcame her when she was around Cyrus.

So what to do about such an actuality?

He wanted to marry someone with power and influence, and while she understood he had his reasons for this, that did not stop how she was starting to feel about the man. Or, more truthfully, how she *felt* about him.

She entered Hyde Park and made her way toward Rotten Row, her groom following behind. Julia sighed, losing herself in the many wonderful, delicious memories of how he had made her feel. His touch, his hands on her body. What they had done. Her shattering climax made her ache even now.

Her stomach fluttered, a pang of renewed need. How

was she to attempt to suit another when all her mind focused on was where Cyrus was at any given moment? Whom he was speaking to? Did he look happy or annoyed? Was he giving any other women more attention than was proper? More attention than herself?

The Dowager Duchess of Barker certainly had made her intentions clear, and although Julia wanted to know if there was more between them than flirtation, she had not asked him last evening.

Rotten Row came into view, and she was glad to see it wasn't as crowded as she had thought it would be, especially with the Season in full swing. She trotted out onto the track, keeping to the edge and out of the way of the men who thought to gallop the length, even though it was not allowed.

At this early hour, other ladies were present, but like herself, they seemed more than happy to keep to themselves and their own musings.

Julia heard the thundering of hooves and turned to watch Lord Chilsten coming toward her. Her mouth dried at the sight of him. He appeared as if he had just rolled out of bed, threw on his shirt, and barely had time to button it up, nevertheless have his valet tie his cravat properly for him.

His jaw was shadowed, proving the point that he had not bathed this morning, and her body thrummed with renewed want of him. Seeing him again, feeling the way she did, as if her heart could burst and her stomach would flutter away like a butterfly, told her even more than before that she could never marry anyone other than the man before her.

But how to convince him of that fact?

He is here, is he not? Has he singled you out once again?

All true, but still, he seemed determined to remain a bachelor, and she wanted a marriage like her sisters enjoyed. She wanted a husband who loved her. Did Cyrus have any feelings for her, or did he merely find her attractive enough to kiss her whenever the opportunity arose?

That, she did not know, but she needed to find out.

"Julia," he said, his use of her given name making her breath catch.

She smiled up at him, his mount puffing and stomping at the abrupt halt from his run.

"You're up early this morning, my lord. One cannot help but think you have not been abed yet." She hoped that was untrue, especially after what they had been up to together at the ball. But he did indeed look as if he had not slept.

He grinned, the devilish look that made her toes curl in her riding boots. "I have slept, and I dreamed of you," he teased her.

She rolled her eyes, walking her horse forward. "You did not dream of me, liar. Maybe the Duchess of Barker, but not me," she suggested, needing to know his intentions with the lady. To hear him say he had not dreamed of the duchess at all...

He laughed, throwing back his head before meeting her eye. "Are you jealous of Her Grace?" He studied her a moment before growing serious. "Do not be. Nothing is going on between the Duchess of Barker and me. I would not be kissing you all over London if that were the case."

His words pleased her, and warmth flooded her veins. "Would you not? You do have a reputation for being a rake. Kissing me would not normally stop you from kissing others unless I have burrowed under your skin so much that I'm all that occupies that rakehell mind of yours."

His eyes grew wide before he reached over, pulling her

mount to a stop. "You are a forward little minx this morning, are you not? Did something happen last evening that makes you voice your opinion so openly?" he queried.

Looking about and seeing no one nearby, she reached out, placing her hand on his thigh, squeezing it a little. "You dreamed of me last night. That is why you look as if you have not slept a wink because I kept you up all night. What did your dream have in it? I'm curious to know, my lord."

He covered her hand with his. It was cool and yet made her blood run hot in her veins. "I did dream of you, and it is by chance that we have met here this morning. I needed to clear my mind, halt the hardness in my breeches before my valet thought I had advances toward him. As for what you did in my dreams, Julia, well..." He slid her hand farther along his thigh, closer to where his manhood jutted against his breeches. "I fucked you as I wanted to last night and enjoyed every delicious orgasm you had while impaled on me."

Julia swallowed. She shifted on the saddle, her cunny ached at his words, and she could feel he had made her wet. Again.

The man was impossible. Hot and cold. Determined to marry but was quite content to torture her with what she wanted but could never have. Well, two could play at his game. She knew to her very core what she wanted, who she wanted to marry, and Lord Chilsten, flirt extraordinaire and debaucher of innocent ladies, was it. She would change his mind and leave him with no other choice but to marry her.

She scoffed, raising her brows at his words. "What a shame it is only a dream, my lord. There is no proof that should we be so intimate," she said, taking her hand back and clasping her reins with a determined grip, "that you would have such success. It is one thing, is it not, to touch, to play, and stroke one's person, but quite another when one does the...deed to have similar success."

He cleared his throat, his lips twitching. "I can assure you, Miss Julia, that I'm more than capable of bringing such enjoyment to you, even when doing the *deed* as you state."

She shrugged, pushing her horse forward into a walk. "What a shame it is that you will never find out the truth of your declaration."

He caught up to her, his eyes twinkling in mirth and determination. She shivered at the sight of him looking down at her as if he wanted to devour her or something. She could imagine what that something was now.

"You taunt me. Has no one ever told you, Miss Julia, that you ought not to poke the hungry lion?"

She laughed, dismissing his words with a wave of her hand. "Really, Lord Chilsten. You are a lark. Now you're a hungry lion? What we have done so far is all that I will allow, which is more than I should have. You are a rake and determined to remain unmarried. I shall have to linger in your dreams, my lord. For you will never have me in truth."

She watched him and did not miss the shadow that clouded his eyes a moment before he blinked, and it was gone. "We're alone, Julia. Why have you reverted to calling me Lord Chilsten?" he asked, throwing her away from what they were discussing.

She looked ahead and noticed they were far from anyone else in the park. "We may be alone, but we're at a public park. Best to keep up the pretense that we're merely friends and nothing more."

"But we are more. Much more," he said, pinning her with his dark, hooded gaze that made her feel warm and delicious.

"No, we are not. Not really. I'm still going to marry

someone else, and it would be pointless for me to continue kissing you. Even if your tutelage is so very helpful in making me understand the type of marriage I would like," she lied, knowing full well she wanted to marry the man at her side and no one else. "Our intimate interludes need to cease, and you need to go back to assisting me with whatever lord catches my eye. Let me know if he's noble and without scandal. I think that is best."

"And if I cannot keep my hands from your person? What then?" he asked her, a muscle in his jaw working under his cheek.

"You will, for I will ensure the opportunity does not arise for us to be alone again." She threw Lord Chilsten a consoling smile. "I'm sorry, my lord, but if you wish to have me in full, you shall have to marry me."

"Are you proposing marriage, Miss Woodville? How very modern of you."

She laughed. "Would you say no if I was?" She pulled her mount to a stop and met his gaze.

His eyes widened a fraction, and his mouth opened and closed several times before finding his voice. "Are you teasing me, Julia?"

She did not look away, wanting him to wonder if she were or were not teasing him. Which, in truth, she was not. He was her match, in all ways. The silly rogue needed to realize that fact himself. And if she had to make him want her so much that he offered marriage, then that is what she would do. "Marry me, Lord Chilsten, and find out if I'm teasing or not at the wedding."

He grinned and laughed, pointing at her as if she'd made a hilarious comment. Of course, she had not, but she would let him think she was teasing. "You have a sense of humor. Men like that, and I like that. You ought to let it be known to the gentlemen who interest you."

She just had, she wanted to scream at him. She had shown him, but hilarious or not, it was what she wanted and what she would get. "I must go, but I shall see you this evening at Lord and Lady Lawrence's ball, yes?"

"Yes, I shall be in attendance. We shall continue your hunt this evening. Good day to you," he said, tipping his hat, his wicked mouth tempting her more than she cared to admit.

"Good day to you too, my lord." Julia pushed her mount into a trot and then a canter as she made her way out of the park. What she had stated was true. She needed to make him so desperate for her that he offered marriage. She was certain that once married to her, his eye would not stray. That his life as one of the worst rakes in London would cease to exist.

She hoped...

CHAPTER
TEN

T rue to her word Julia had not allowed another evening to descend into them being alone or having at it with each other in a darkened drawing room. Much to his annoyance, she allowed a bevy of men to court her, her tinkling laugh making the hair on his skin stand on end.

The many dances she had that were not with him were too many to count, and worse, some of those interactions he could see she enjoyed and welcomed the gentleman's suit.

It had been almost two weeks since their interlude in the vacant drawing room at the masked ball, and it was too long. It wasn't to be borne. He could not sleep for the thought of her. She invaded his dreams and taunted him senseless with images of her joining him in his bed, lying beside him, and giving herself to him, welcoming his touch.

And damn it all to hell, he wanted to touch her.

And he certainly did not want anyone else to touch her in his place.

But what to do about it? He knew what he ought to do,

but to take that leap was another thing altogether. Would she welcome his hand? How would he tell her the truth of his marriage and the child that resulted from it? Julia Woodville was kind. Hell, the family was known for their warmth toward others. Would that understanding nature extend to a rake who got a maid with child?

He rubbed a hand over his jaw, debating what to do. She was no society's diamond. She was an heiress, but with few connections other than her sister's grand matches. That was something he supposed... Better than what she would have been had her sisters merely married untitled gentlemen.

But would she be high enough in society to withstand the fallout of his actions when they became known? And he knew they would one day. It was only a matter of time. Nothing remained a secret in the *ton*, and certainly, a gentleman who slept with his servant was fodder for those who lived for gossip.

Julia would have to sail those stormy seas by his side and forgive him his sin. He had made a mistake, but he could not regret the child that had come from that error. She was the most adorable little cherub, and he would send for her to return to him in England as soon as he had secured a bride.

His attention flittered across the ballroom before stopping on the Dowager Duchess of Barker. She was a widowed duchess. High enough in the peerage to look down on anyone who said a word out of place about her husband or his foibles. He knew she was back in London, searching for a new husband or lover, whatever came first. She would marry him and stomach any scandalous past he owned after the fact. But she also wasn't the woman he yearned for.

Cyrus looked back to where Julia had been a moment before and caught her watching him, an annoyed look to her normally pretty visage. Had she caught him observing the dowager duchess? Was she envious? He hoped she was and that what he felt wasn't solely his condition to withstand.

Julia started to move through the throng of guests, coming to join him soon after. She glanced up at him, a mocking twist to her lips. "Still pining for the dowager duchess, I see. Do not worry, my lord, your assistance with me will soon be over, and you shall be able to marry your lover."

He frowned down at her, watching her until she deemed him worthy of meeting his eye. "What makes you think she's my lover?"

"The other week on the Serpentine, you looked quite the cozy couple, out boating, laughing, and being all too familiar. There would be few who would not think that was the case."

"You and I have been intimate since then. Do you think I play several women at one time? You do not have a high opinion of me." The thought that she would think that left him cold, and a hard knot settled in the pit of his gut.

"Are you telling me you have not thought about sleeping with the dowager duchess? I'm certain from how she is looking at you even now that she would welcome you into her bed."

Cyrus was unsure what had spiked this temper in Julia, but he also liked her fiery spirit. She would be a good match for him, keep him on his toes. Something he worried about when choosing a wife, or at least when he picked one not forced on him by his own misdeeds. He had expected to marry someone he did not care too much about when he did find an appropriate wife to weather the storm that was coming with his truth. But he could not say that about the woman at his side.

He cared for Julia and looked for her at every ball and party. When he could not see her in attendance, all the evening's enjoyment dissipated with that truth.

"She may welcome me, and there may have been a time that I would have lain beside her. But not anymore."

The words, marry me, sat on the tip of his tongue, yet he could not voice them.

"Oh really? Has someone else crossed your path, and the rake in you growled in approval?"

What was happening here? Why was she being so dismissive of him all of a sudden? Could she not read between his words and realize he spoke of her, that she was the woman that occupied all his thoughts. "Apologies if I have offended you in some way, Miss Julia, but I thought we were friends. Has something happened that I'm not aware of that has put you against me?" he asked, pinning her to the spot.

Her lips thinned into a displeased line, and he thought hard on what it could have been that had made her so off toward him this evening. They had an agreement, did they not? He would help her, and she would marry another. That had not changed, at least not outwardly.

But he had changed and no longer wanted that for either of them, and he would tell her soon. He had to, for he could not go on for much longer without having her in his arms again. Even now, with her annoyed and flushed beside him, her hands fisted and her brow furrowed in annoyance, he wanted her. He wanted to wrench her into his arms and kiss her sweet lips, taste her desire, and revel in the feel of her touch on his skin. Declare before all of

London that Julia Woodville was his and no one, not Lord Perry or Mr. Watts or the dreaded Lord Payne, had a chance of winning her hand.

For he had won her and would marry her. Make her the next Marchioness of Chilsten and Scottish Duchess of Rothes.

"No, we are still friends, but that is all, and that is how it will stay. I have decided to allow Lord Perry to call on me at home. We're taking a carriage ride out to the old castle ruins near Richmond, and then we're going to Gunter's for tea and cake afterward. You never know, Lord Chilsten. This time tomorrow evening, I may be betrothed, and your helping me will no longer be required, but I shall always be thankful."

Anger thrummed through him at the mention of her planned outing. So many opportunities for Lord Perry to touch her. Steal a kiss. Offer to marry her. "You would not accept his offer straightaway, surely? You do not even know the man. He could—"

"I know him as much as I know you, but he is a gentleman unlike you, Lord Chilsten," she interrupted. "He may not have kissed me as you have, but I think that honorable, not something to be pitied. I know you do not know how to be around a woman without needing to pet them somehow, but not all men are like you. Thankfully," she added, her pert little nose rising in the air as if she had finished with her point.

He ground his teeth, unable to tear his gaze from her. "He could be cruel, and you would not know until you were married. Do not act in haste simply because you're angry with me for something."

"And why am I angry with you? I have nothing to be angry about," she stated, a rosy hue kissing her cheeks. He had seen her color rise before, but in the throes of passion, and it reminded him of the last time they were alone. Made the desperation within him rise up to be almost wild in nature.

"I know your secret, Julia, for it is the same as mine." There he had said it. Her mouth opened with a gasp, and it took all of his strength not to kiss her in the ballroom. Take her lips and drink from her, soothe the parched desperation within him. Soothe her ire.

"Our secret is the same? I do not believe that is true," she teased, her tone mocking.

"You're jealous, Julia. Jealous the dowager duchess may seduce me to her bed. That it will not be you who warms my silk sheets night after night but her. I know this is so, for I do not want to see you anywhere near Lord Perry. I do not want to hear of you riding with him, having tea at Gunter's. The thought of you kissing him sends me into a spiral of panic and hate. I want to pummel his lordship to a pulp while also congratulating him for winning you."

She stared up at him as if he had grown a second head, and in truth, he wasn't sure that he had not. He had never been so honest, so brutal with his words to mean what he said. He met her gaze, held it, and hoped that she would not laugh or dismiss what he said.

Instead, she fled. Pushed past him, and before he could see where she had gone, she had disappeared into the throng of guests. Not an easy feat due to her height. He moved in the direction she went, needing to find her, if only to ensure she was well and that his honesty had not hurt her.

He spotted her heading to the foyer. The crush of the ball made catching up to her difficult, and it wasn't until she was stepping up into the ducal carriage that he finally made her side. "You're leaving?" he asked.

She did not look at him, merely stepped up with the footman's help, who then tried to close the door in his face. "Excuse me, lad, but I haven't finished talking to Miss Woodville."

The footman looked to Julia, who nodded her approval, giving him his way. Without thought, he stepped up into the vehicle and banged on the roof, signaling for them to leave. The carriage lurched forward. The only sound to be heard was the wheels on the cobbled street and the fading notes of the ball as they left.

"Are you quite content, my lord? You should not be in here with me."

He ran a hand through his hair, fighting to control what he felt for the woman before him. "Admit what I said is true. I cannot be the only one inflicted with this... With this..."

She raised one brow mockingly. "With feelings, my lord? I know you do not suffer from such ailments often, but is that what you're trying to say?"

"You vex me and mock what I'm trying to import to you. I know you want me as much as I want you. Admit it."

"I think you forget something important and necessary for me to admit such feelings, my lord. I shall wait until you say what I want to hear before giving you my opinion."

He gaped at her. Was she serious? What more did she want him to do? Beg? Get on one knee? The thought of kneeling before her in a carriage had merit, and now that he had thought of it, he wanted that more than anything right now.

He slipped off the seat, clutching her long, lean thighs. Thighs he wanted to kiss after having her over his lap.

Cyrus leaned down, kissing her knee, covered by yards of green silk and smelling of sweet lilies. He felt her shiver under his touch, and it wasn't enough. He needed her. Existing these past two weeks without her had been torture and one he did not want to repeat.

"Do you have any idea what I want to do to you, Julia?" he asked, no longer too proud to say how much he desired her and enjoyed her.

She stared down at him, her eyes glistening with desire. She bit her lip, shaking her head. "Will you tell me?" she asked.

Cyrus did not think he could grow any harder for her, but he did at her sultry, whispered words. He closed his eyes a moment, steeling himself not to lose control. He grinned, slipping her gown up her thighs to reveal her thin, silk-clad thighs. "No, my darling. I'm not going to tell you anything, but I will show you. With my mouth."

CHAPTER
ELEVEN

Julia bit her lip. Watched, enthralled, as Cyrus pushed her gown up to pool at her waist, exposing her unmentionables and much more than that to his inspection. Wickedness crossed his features, and she wondered what he was going to do.

"Did you know that a woman can have just as much pleasure wrought upon her as a man and without the need for intercourse?" he said, pushing her thighs apart.

Julia felt heat kiss her cheeks but, too gripped by what he was saying and doing, she did not try to halt his intent. Her body no longer felt as if it were hers. Fire coursed through her blood. She wanted to wiggle, move closer to his intoxicating mouth that teased her mercilessly with his words.

"A little," she admitted. "You have shown me some of what I can have." And she wanted more. So much more of what he could give her.

He growled, dipping his head to kiss just above her silk stocking on her thigh. Goosebumps rose on her skin, and she clutched the cushions beside her. "What else is there that you can do?" she asked, needing to know—wanting him to do everything that her imagination could think of.

He pushed her legs farther apart, exposing her wet mons to his view. She ought to be horrified, scandalized by the liberties she was giving him, but she was not. A little embarrassed, yes, but her need overrode all nerves, and she was left with nothing but wanting him.

His lips kissed their way along her thigh, his warm breath making her shiver. His fingers ran along her sex, and she swallowed a moan as desire pooled where his fingers teased. He slipped within her, a slow, maddening stroke that made her want to scream. "This is how I'll fuck you, Julia, without ever compromising you."

She lay her head against the squabs, closed her eyes, and gave herself to what he was doing to her. His mumbled words of perfection, of her sweet taste, floated to her ears. All of it was lost to her, for all she could do was breathe, to hold on, and stop herself from shouting out that she wanted more. So much more than this.

As delightful as this was, she wanted him—all of him, no matter the consequences.

"What else can you do, my lord?" she asked, cringing at the desperation that tinged her tone.

He pulled his fingers from her, meeting her gaze. Transfixed, she watched as he slipped his digits into his mouth, relishing her taste as if eating some sweet dessert. "You're fucking delicious."

She squirmed, impatient for more. "Is there more?" she asked, knowing from the burning light in his eyes that there was.

"So much more," he said, dipping his head to where his fingers were a moment before. She gasped, clutched at his hair, and held him. She wasn't sure whether to push him away or pull him closer before his tongue flicked across a delightful spot on her that sent her wits reeling.

"Cyrus," she cried, her legs spreading, letting him have at her in any way he wished. The action was wanton, scandalous, but she did not care so long as he continued what he had started.

He sucked on her, and she bucked, having never felt such an intoxicating, enthralling feeling before. His mouth was everywhere, kissing, lathing, sucking, and teasing her relentlessly. She moaned his name, undulated against his mouth, heedless of how she appeared, so long as he continued what he was doing.

Pleasure taunted her, ebbed and flowed through her like a tide. Over and over, he kissed her there, his fingers sometimes joining his mouth. Pressure built deep within her core, release was close, and she wanted it with a desperation verging on nonsensical.

"Please, Cyrus. Please, give me what I want," she begged of him, mindless with the need for what she knew he could give her.

He hoisted her legs atop his shoulders, pulling her down on the squabs and coming over her farther, kissing her deeper with frantic strokes. She rolled her head from side to side, holding on to him in fear of losing herself beyond this earth.

How was it that such wickedness could be so good?

And then she felt the first tremors rushing through her cunny, outwardly into her body, through every part of her. She covered her mouth with her hand, moaning his name as convulsion after convulsion transported her to a utopia of pleasure.

She opened her eyes to find him kissing her leg, slowly working his way away from her mons while placing her gown back over her knees. He sat back on his heels, his color high, the bulge in his breeches even higher.

She came down onto the carriage floor with him, wrapping her arms about his neck. "I want to give you pleasure. Let me give you what you just gave to me," she begged, knowing that it must be the same for him if it were possible to do such a thing to her.

He gave her a small smile but shook his head. "We're almost back to the Derby town house, and you ought to go home before anyone sees you being taken home in a carriage with me. If we remain here for much longer, I shall allow you to do what you wish, and it is not right. Not yet."

She shivered at his words. Wanted to push him more to see if she could get what she desired.

Just at that moment, the carriage rolled to a halt, and disappointment left a sour taste in her mouth. "I cannot be home so soon. I do not want to leave you," she admitted, hoping she was not too forward. She was supposed to make him long for her and want her and no one else. Not hand herself over like a sweet meat for consumption.

Her self-control had failed her the first moment it was tested.

"We have time, Julia," he said, helping her back onto the seat just as the door opened. The footman let down the steps, and Julia reluctantly stepped down. She turned and found Cyrus seated where he was before, the respectable lord once again. Even though only a moment before, he had been anything but.

"St. James Square," he called out to the driver as the duke's footman shut the door. Julia met his eyes and saw that he was determined to leave. She turned on her heel, going inside, needing to plan and think more about how she would get her little plan back into motion. The carriage rolled down the street, and she denied herself from watching him depart into the night. She was going on an outing with Lord Perry tomorrow. She would ensure it was successful and that word of her success got back to Cyrus. Making him jealous seemed the only way to make him act. And hopefully, after tomorrow, he would.

CHAPTER
TWELVE

T he following morning the carriage arrived for Julia on time and as planned with Lord Perry. She greeted him before the ducal town house, pleased to be outdoors today since the weather was warm and calm, a perfect day to explore old castle ruins.

Julia took Lord Perry's outstretched hand and climbed up onto the Barouche. Her maid followed soon after and jumped up to sit beside the driver.

"Good day, Miss Julia. How very delightful our afternoon will be, do you not think?" Lord Perry asked, informing the driver to start their journey.

She sat on the seat and settled her skirts. "I think the excursion will be pleasant indeed. How long do you think it shall take us to reach the castle ruins?"

He leaned back in the seat, smiling. "An hour, no more. Many Londoners travel out to Richmond to the park and go on to see the ruins. I should not think we will be alone," he said, grinning at her as if he knew a secret she did not.

Julia nodded, but did not react to his words. She did like Lord Perry, but she would not marry him. There was only one man she wished to marry, and after today, she would cool her association with his lordship. He did not deserve to be a pawn in the game she played with Lord Chilsten.

"My maid is looking forward to the day as much as myself," she reminded him.

He cast a look ahead, and distaste crossed his face. She watched him, wondering how changeable he was since the ball when he invited her out on this adventure. What was wrong with the man to be so odd toward her chaperone?

"Do you often care what your servants think? I know I do not."

Julia swallowed her fiery retort and hoped Masie had not heard what he had said. Her maid was a widow and a respectable woman. Such words would hurt her. "I will not be cruel or severe to anyone if I can help it. I think more people should aspire to such manners. Do you not think?" she asked him, hoping this change of temperament was merely nerves and he would not be so disagreeable all day.

He shrugged, his mouth turned down into a displeased smile. "I shall not be cruel or hurtful to you, Miss Julia. I only want to make your day pleasant and full of fun and laughter." He gestured to a basket at their feet. "I had my cook pack a picnic should we need to break our fast. I hope you like pork pie."

Julia closed her eyes, the mere thought of eating pig wanting to make her cast up her accounts. She had never liked the taste of the flesh, and to have that as the only offering would be torture indeed. "I shall have a look at what your cook has prepared. I'm certain there will be something that will tempt me."

The carriage headed southwest out of the city, and they were soon in the countryside. Lord Perry was correct, other carriages were on the road, but they could also be traveling east to Bath.

"I've been noted as quite the host, and I'm certain you shall enjoy the pork pies. I serve them often at events I host. They are a favorite of mine, after all."

Julia fought not to roll her eyes. She would not be marrying Lord Perry, if only because he ate pig. She shuddered and looked ahead. "The road is quite dusty, is it not, with all the carriages and horses."

"It is, but we shall be turning just ahead, and then we shall not be far from the castle."

Excellent, because now that she was on this afternoon jaunt, she could not wait for it to be over. The sooner they arrived, inspected the ruins, and ate the awful lunch that awaited her, the sooner they would return to London.

The man beside her was nothing like the gentleman who complimented and spoke of interesting things at the last ball where they were together. This man seemed a little cold, dismissing her maid, and bossy. No one wanted to be told they had to eat a certain food. She was not five and under a nanny's tutelage.

"There it is." Julia pointed to the circular part of the ruin quickly glimpsed through the trees. She leaned forward, touching her maid to show her. "Look, Masie, there it is. I shall have much to tell Hailey this evening, how majestic it is."

Her maid nodded, and Julia smiled, excited to study the ruins as they approached. Lord Perry cleared his throat. "Your maid may wait at the carriage while we walk the ruins."

Julia stilled at his cold words, and nor would she listen to such ideals. For propriety's sake, she needed Masie with her, even if she did wish to be alone with his lordship, which she did not. "Masie will be joining me, my lord. I will not be leaving her at the carriage. She's my chaperone," she reminded him.

A muscle worked in his jaw, and she could not fathom why having her maid with her would irritate him so. It was commonplace for unmarried women to bring their maids. Unless... She swallowed, the pit of her stomach tied in knots. He had brought her here today to try to force her hand somehow. Her brother-in-law, the duke, said it wasn't unheard of for heiresses to be compromised. Maybe she should not have come.

"If you wish it," he said, giving her a small smile.

Julia nodded, knowing that it was what she wished and what would occur. His attempt at appeasing her did not work, and nerves took hold and would not abate.

The carriage started up a small incline. At the top, there seemed to be a clearing for carriages and horses to be parked for those who wished to explore the castle. No other carriages were present, nor horses, which made her more uneasy.

The wheel hit a divot in the road, and a crack sounded right before the carriage lurched to one side. Her maid gasped, and Julia clutched the side of the carriage to stop herself from falling into Lord Perry's lap. The horses jumped forward, the broken wheel startling them a little, but thankfully the driver settled the mounts and stopped them from bolting while still attached to the equipage.

They pulled up, the carriage on a terrible lean that made disembarking hard. "The wheel has broken clean off," Lord Perry said, his voice as startled as his face. "That is unexpected."

Very, Julia thought, holding the side and trying not to slide into Lord Perry. "Can you help me down, my lord?" she asked, wanting off the vehicle, not trusting the horses not to bolt since they seemed less than settled, still hitched as they were. "Jump down, Masie," she instructed her maid.

Lord Perry helped her down, his arm going about her waist and pushing up against her breasts in the most unpleasant way. She ignored the heat that flashed in his eyes and merely moved out of his hold as quickly as possible.

When the ground met her leather boots, she sighed in relief, going to her maid, who kept a safe distance from the carriage.

Lord Perry jumped down and inspected the carriage, now absent of one wheel, before helping the driver unhitch the horses. "I shall have to ride back to London with my driver and bring another carriage out to you. You may look at the ruins and have the picnic I had packed. I shall return by the time you have done all of that."

Julia looked to Masie and did not miss the worry in her eyes. "Very well, my lord. But please make haste. It is not safe for us to be out here alone without a male escort." The thought of running into a highwayman or thieves or worse, people she did not want even to contemplate, made her stomach coil in dread.

"I will be but two hours, Miss Julia. Do not worry," Lord Perry said, walking the horses out of the hitching rails and away from the broken carriage. He tied the mounts to a tree and then went back to the carriage, taking out the picnic basket that had sat at their feet.

"Here is your lunch. I believe on the other side of the castle ruins, there is a river if you wish to cool the ratafia I had bottled for our trip."

"Thank you, my lord," she said, taking the basket from him and watching as he and his driver jumped upon the saddleless horses, turning them back toward the direction they had traveled. She reached out just before he started off, taking the horse's reins and stopping him. "Maybe this is the wrong choice. I'm certain there will be others having an excursion here today. Maybe we all wait together, ask for them to return us to London instead of you leaving us here."

He laughed, leaning down and patting her cheek. She reeled back from his touch, unsure why he had touched her so inappropriately. "Do not worry, Miss Julia. Nothing will happen to you. I shall be back before I am missed."

Julia stepped back, watching both men trot down the hill. She turned to Masie and stared at her for a long moment, unsure they had actually been left alone to defend themselves in the middle of nowhere.

"Come, Miss Julia. We shall go to the ruins, find a place to break our fast. A less-visible place before we decide on what we're to do."

Julia nodded, following her maid, who picked up the basket before heading down to the ruins. Had Julia wanted to explore the location, it would have been marvelous, but her mind and stomach would not settle or stop racing with worry now that they were alone.

It took them an hour to ride out to this location, and therefore to walk back to London would take them several. Neither her boots nor her maid's shoes were sturdy enough for such a long trek. Not to mention who knew who they would run into on the Bath road. Their savior may not be so savory at all.

Julia nodded and followed her maid down a worn path that led to the castle nestled at the bottom of a small hill. A river did indeed run on the opposite side, and they were able to find makeshift seats close to the water but hidden from view from anyone who may explore the ruins later that day.

"If someone arrives, we will watch them for a moment and then gauge whether it would be safe for us to speak to them. Mayhap we can ask for a lift back to London should they be going in that direction. We are bound to cross paths with Lord Perry on his return, and he will stop to follow us home."

Masie rummaged in the basket, pulling out the bottle of ratafia and some bread wrapped in cloth. "Here, Miss Julia. Have something to eat. I'm certain Lord Perry will do as he stated and return in a specified time. We should look about the ruins and not let this incident ruin our outing."

What her maid said made sense, but still, Julia did not like to be alone. They were vulnerable here without protection. Not that she necessarily needed a man to be such to her, but a flintlock would be handy right now.

Even so, for over an hour, they walked through the ruins, marveling at the once-grand structure. Now nothing but a shell of what it once may have been. They found a safe picnic area near the water's edge, but no one arrived to sightsee such as they had. The day was eerily quiet and put her on guard.

"We have been out here for over two hours, Masie. Should not Lord Perry have returned by now?"

Her maid looked in the direction that carriages would arrive, her brow furrowed. "I do not know why he is not back. Mayhap it took longer to source another carriage. I'm certain he should not be far away."

Julia was not so sure, and the pit of her stomach churned. Something was not right. But then, Lord Perry did not know his carriage wheel would break, so there was no reason why he would not return.

If only he would, so they could leave. She shivered as the sun dipped beneath the tree line. He needed to return before they spent a night out in the woods with nothing but their useless day dresses and shawls to keep them warm.

Which would not keep them warm at all.

THIRTEEN

L ord Chilsten arrived at the Duke of Derby's Berkeley Square town house wanting to call on Derby, and if by chance he ran into Miss Julia, then all the better. A smile lifted his lips as the memory of their last time together floated through his mind.

He handed the footman his hat and gloves and stilled at the sound of the duchess's concerned tone coming from the library.

"Wait here if you please," the butler said, heading toward the library door just as it opened, and the duke strode purposefully out into the foyer. He skidded to a stop, the duchess hot on his heels, almost running into his back.

"Chilsten," he said, coming up and shaking his hand. "I'm in a hurry, but I shall be at our club later this evening if you wish to catch up then," he said, calling for his carriage.

"Of course," Cyrus said, noting the duchess's pale countenance. "I hope everything is well?"

The duke took his greatcoat from a footman, his wife helping him into it. "It's Miss Julia. She has not returned from her outing this morning with Lord Perry. They traveled out to the castle ruins near Richmond with her maid but have not yet returned. They are long past due."

A cold knot settled in his gut, his skin prickled in unease. "Do you think something has happened to the vehicle? There is no reason why they would not be back as yet. Are you not dining at Lord and Lady Shaw's home this evening before the ball?"

"We are, and when she did not return in time to prepare for dinner, the duchess informed me of her concern. It is odd and not usual of her behavior."

The duchess sniffed, and Cyrus noted her upset. "I shall come with you. I have my carriage outside, and it is big enough should they need an escort home."

"That is the thing," the duke said, frowning at his wife before bussing her cheek and whispering something in her ear. "Lord Perry has been seen back in town this afternoon. The duchess's lady's maid was on errands and spotted Lord Perry in St. James, but no sign of Julia or her maid. I sent a footman to inquire, but he has not been able to locate Lord Perry."

"Let us go now. We only have an hour, two at the most before it is full dark."

"Yes," the duke said, following him.

Cyrus told his driver of their location and the haste in which to head out of London, and they were soon heading west toward Richmond. Cyrus watched as the city gave way to green pastures and trees, the lands and the animals that lived upon them settling down for the night.

The thought of Julia and her maid out in such conditions without protection left him cold. "What would Lord Perry's purpose be to leave them at the ruins if they are indeed there? Would they have returned to London, and you merely do not know it?"

The duke shook his head. "No, Julia is a level-headed woman. She would not worry her sister so, but I could not tell you as for Lord Perry's purpose. He has asked me for Julia's hand, but mayhap he does not want to wait the month required for the banns to be called."

"You have given him permission to marry her?" Cyrus asked, seriously contemplating what he would do should the duke want such a match. He knew he would have to marry a woman of status and influence one day, but he did not want Julia to marry either. He was selfish enough to want them both to remain just as they were right now and commit to no one.

You cannot continue skipping close to ruin with her. She deserves much better than that.

The duke nodded but looked less than pleased by the notion. "I have, of course. Lord Perry is respectable and has no debt or scandal attached to his name. Not that it will make a difference to Miss Julia. When I told her of Lord Perry's request, she laughed and stated he could ask but that it did not mean she had to say yes. It will take a strong-willed and patient man to marry my darling wife's sister. I love her. She's possibly my favorite of them all, but what a handful. I wish anyone luck who desires her as his wife."

Cyrus's lips twitched. She was a delightful, delectable handful whom he wanted in his arms always.

"Does the carriage have blankets? They will be chilled through if they are indeed stranded at the ruins."

"I do, several under the squabs."

"Very good." The duke shook his head, lost in thought. "To ruin her and force her hand Lord Perry would need to return to town with her past a respectable hour. If anyone saw them, a maid in tow or not, late at night, there would not be much we could do to save her reputation. But he is in London. Leaving them there makes no sense at all."

"It does not, but we shall be there soon enough, and let us hope first and foremost that they are safe and well. Then we shall seek the answers to our questions." Either way, Lord Perry had a lot of explaining to do and not only to the duke but to Cyrus too. If he found out the bastard sought to take Julia's choice away, he would pummel him to a pulp.

Julia wrapped her maid in her arms as the sun finally dipped behind the hill. A magical, interesting sight only hours before, now, the ruins looked foreboding, cold, looming over them like doom.

"I do not understand why Lord Perry did not return. Why leave us here?" her maid said for the hundredth time, and still, Julia did not have an answer for her.

"I do not know, Masie." The chill of the air kissed her skin, and she tried to huddle them both under her light shawl as best she could, but it was no use. They would freeze if they did not do something.

"Come, we will walk. It will keep us warm, and we shall have more chance of hitching a ride back to London on the road than here at the ruins."

"But Miss Julia, what if we come upon someone who wishes to do us harm? What will we do?"

Julia looked about as best she could in the dying light. "We shall pick up two big sticks and hold them. Be prepared to use them as a weapon. Other than that, I do not know what to do. Neither of us can start a fire to keep us warm through the night."

Her maid started sobbing at her words, and Julia

rubbed her back. "It'll be well, Masie. Do not worry. I shall get you home soon and safe. Do not become upset."

"Julia!"

She gasped at the sound of her name called in the familiar tone she knew as well as her own. "Lord Chilsten!" she called back. "We're down here," she shouted, helping her maid to stand as they started out of their hiding location.

Feet crunching on gravel and broken brambles sounded through the dark. Just as they stepped out of the trees, hiding them from view, Julia spotted Lord Chilsten and her brother-in-law, the duke, striding in their direction.

Without thought, Julia ran into Cyrus's embrace, welcoming his strong arms that came about her. She clutched tight onto him, forgetting that the duke was watching her every move. She felt the brush of Lord Chilsten's lips atop her head before he pulled her back, staring down at her.

They were safe at last.

And Cyrus looked furious.

CHAPTER FOURTEEN

"What happened that you're out here alone? Derby mentioned you were on an outing with Lord Perry?"

Julia stepped out of his hold, righting herself and taking a deep breath. One that felt like the first in as many hours. They were safe. Derby would take her home to her sister, and this nightmare excursion would finally be over.

"Lord Perry picked us up before luncheon today for a visit to these ruins, but upon arrival, the carriage wheel broke. He went back to fetch another carriage but did not return."

The duke frowned at Chilsten before coming forward and taking her arm. "Come, Julia, we'll return you home to Hailey. She's terribly worried and upset."

Julia nodded, starting for the carriage. Soon they were all ensconced and on their way back to London. Julia shivered into her shawl, the night growing chillier the darker it became. "Did you happen upon Lord Perry on your way out to collect us? Do you think something happened to him, and that is why he did not return?"

The driver hollered outside before the carriage rocked to a halt. Julia met her maid's startled eyes, but before she could look to see what was happening, the duke and Lord Chilsten were tumbling out of the vehicle.

"Bandits?" her maid gasped, her eyes wide with alarm.

Julia slid toward the window and glanced out. Anger replaced the fear that had coursed through her at the sight of Lord Perry jumping down from his mount. The sickening sound of fist meeting flesh sounded on the air, and she stared, wide-eyed at the sight of Lord Chilsten knocking Lord Perry directly on his nose.

The man went down, clasping his face and bellowing a multitude of insults toward Cyrus.

"How dare you strike me," he said, getting to his feet and starting toward the marquess. Derby stepped between them, pushing Lord Perry aside.

"How dare I? How dare you leave two women alone and defenseless in the woods."

Julia narrowed her eyes, not certain she liked being termed defenseless. She was going to pick up a stick after all, and she was certain she would know how to whack at something should the need arise. Even so, she remained silent, waiting to see how Lord Perry would explain his way out of his actions.

"I needed to source another carriage."

"And that took all afternoon and into the evening? I shudder at the thought of what could have happened to them had they been out here all night. Do you have any notion of how dangerous your actions were here today?" Cyrus yelled, the anger thrumming off him, making Julia's heart kick up a beat.

"I came as soon as I could," Lord Perry defended.

"That is not true. My wife's lady's maid saw you enter Whites. Explain that, if you will?"

"I did not have another carriage myself. I had to borrow Lord Roberts'," he said, his gaze moving to her.

"You ought to have come to me," the duke said. "Why did you not, unless this was all a plan for you to arrive late at night in London? Or not to return until the wee hours of the morning where my hand may be forced to adhere to society's rules and demand you offer marriage to Miss Julia. Was that what you were trying, Lord Perry?"

"I would not dare," he stuttered. Julia could see Lord Perry's color rise high in the light from the carriage's lanterns, even from where she sat. "I do not need to trick Miss Julia into marriage to win her hand."

Cyrus ran a hand through his hair, pacing. "You will never win her hand, and you will never be alone with her or take her anywhere again. Do you understand?"

Lord Perry put his hands on his hips, affronted. "And who do you think you are, ordering me over a woman who, if I'm not mistaken, is not your wife? You had one of those. Mayhap if you cared for her more, she would still be alive."

Had Julia blinked, she would have missed the second punch that flicked out, striking Lord Perry on the chin. His head snapped back, and he stumbled, but did not fall to the ground.

"Do not speak of my family, or you shall not get up again, Lord Perry. Not ever, mayhap."

Julia bit her lip, having never seen Cyrus so high of emotion, angry and concerned all at once. And mostly because of her.

"Enough now," the duke said, pulling Cyrus away. He glared at Perry, both men looking as if they wanted to murder each other at that moment.

"You will not go near Miss Julia again. Do you under-stand?" the duke stated, his tone brooking no argument.

"I think that is up to the lady herself," Perry pushed back, determined, it would seem, not to allow anyone to order him about. "She has been, after all, out alone, and for all society knows, she's been with me. You may have no choice but to hear of our impending marriage."

Julia gasped. Was this what Perry had planned all along?

Cyrus laughed, pushing the duke's hold away. He adjusted his greatcoat, standing to his full height and towering over Lord Perry, who seemed to shrink at his stance. "Miss Julia will not be marrying you or anyone else, for she will be marrying me before I allow her to throw herself at your feet."

Marry Cyrus? He had not asked her and had stated up to this point that he required a woman of rank, not a gently bred young lady from the country.

What had changed his mind?

Her outing today certainly should not have been enough. She had been chaperoned, after all, and even without a male escort, no one had come upon them who could talk unless Lord Perry had become vocal about the event.

"Miss Julia, did Lord Chilsten propose?" her maid asked her, her eyes still wide, but now because of a new reason.

Julia sat back against the seat, not sure what was happening. She wanted Lord Chilsten, that she had no doubt, but she wanted him to want her too and not merely be the savior to her troubles should any arise after today's predicament.

She wanted him to love her. To fall in love with her. To be with her and no other. He was a rake, his reputation one of the worst in London, if not all of England itself. Would he be faithful? Could he learn to love her and build a life together?

"If one could call it a proposal," she said, just as the carriage door opened and Derby and Chilsten stepped up and took their seats across from Julia and her maid. She watched Lord Perry dust down his jacket, walking back to the carriage he had brought out to collect them. He watched her ride past, and Julia turned away from him. The man had left them for longer than was necessary. He could have hired a hackney if his excuse to get another carriage were true. With enough blunt offered, any hackney would have traveled out to the ruins. They were not too far from the city after all.

Julia's attention moved across the darkened space, and her eyes met Lord Chilsten's. He watched her, and she could see that he wanted to say something, but they were not alone.

"Do not worry, Julia. There will be no scandal from today's failed excursion," the duke said, throwing her a small smile.

She nodded, hoping that was true. "And what of your proposal, Lord Chilsten? Did you mean what you said on the road just before? I do not believe you have asked me to be your wife, yet you seem to think and are willing to declare that we're to be married."

The duke cleared his throat, and Julia ignored the amused grin on his face he was trying to hide from them all.

Cyrus's eyes darkened in determination, and she watched him, not willing to let his handsome, roguish wiles make her swoon at his feet as she tended to do. She often forgot her plans when around him, and he ended up being the one who led them on this merry dance they had been partaking in these past weeks.

"I think you should accept my offer of marriage. Lord Perry will likely be quite put out after my set down this evening. He will be looking to make a point at getting back at me, and through you, no doubt. I will not allow him to sully your name, and therefore I think a marriage between us is necessary."

"So this is you asking me to marry you then?" she asked, her tone sweet, but she was feeling anything but delighted at the prospect. She did not want to marry him because they had an impending scandal or because he felt morally obliged. "You do not want to marry me. You have told me yourself you are looking for a wife of rank, for whatever reason it is that you have not disclosed. Why offer your neck on such a guillotine?"

Cyrus cleared his throat. "I also do not want you to marry Perry."

"So, you're proposing out of jealousy and not wanting anyone else to have me. Is that correct, my lord?" Julia shook her head, not willing to marry anyone under such circumstances. Even if the thought of being Cyrus's wife had its advantages and was something she had longed for since their first kiss a year before. But if he did not love her, she would have little hope of keeping him loyal, and a marriage where she played second to a whore's bed or some other matron of the *ton* would not suit.

"We will discuss the matter when you're safe home at Derby's town house," Cyrus said, dismissing her question.

She narrowed her eyes, not mistaking his authority over her that she was loath to allow. A marriage would be a part-nership, a mutual understanding of love and friendship.

She would not be told again by him, not as a friend or a wife.

"Very well," she conceded. "When we're back at the town house, I request a word with Chilsten, Your Grace. Alone. Will you allow it?"

The duke met her eyes before his attention flicked to Chilsten's. His mouth narrowed in a disapproving line before he nodded. "Very well, but not for long. Do you both agree?" he asked.

"Agreed," they said in unison.

FIFTEEN

The moment the carriage rocked to a halt before the Derby town house was the first time that Cyrus felt as though he could breathe. Julia and her maid were safe. Nothing untoward had happened to them, and they were home without nary a scratch or scandal.

It was a fortunate conclusion. It could have ended with her betrothed to Lord Perry, with nothing that he nor Derby could do about it.

Derby gestured for them to use his library for their discussion. Cyrus bade Julia to go before him as he followed her into the room, its abundance of books and warm evening fire a welcoming reprieve after the chill carriage ride they had just endured the past hour.

He followed her to the hearth, staring at the flames a moment and drinking in the warmth it provided on his person. "What were you thinking going on an outing with Perry with only your maid as a chaperone? You're an heiress. Many men such as Perry could use a situation like you handed his lordship to force a marriage you do not wish for. He left you and did not return, making you vulnerable to unknown danger and the *ton*'s love of gossip. You could be at this very moment entering into an understanding with him. Is that what you want?" he asked her, his anger at the whole situation making his words blunter than he intended.

"You forget, my lord, that I had permission from the duke and my sister to go. That the wheel broke was not something anyone could foresee. While I do not know if Lord Perry changed his mind to use the incident to his advantage, you chastising me over today's events is not welcome. You are not my guardian or my parent. You offered to help me find a gentleman free from scandal, and thankfully I have picked several out that you have said are suitable. You being here, scolding me for a situation out of my control reeks of a man who is overstepping his bounds."

She went to push past him, and he grabbed her hand, wrenching her into him. The feel of her, her scent, her wide, pretty eyes made him ache, and he knew she was right. All of what she said was true. He was berating her, and it was not his place. Nor did she deserve it. But the thought of her being married off to the likes of Perry made his stomach lurch.

"I do not mean to chastise you, Julia. I was worried, that is all."

"Why were you so worried? Is there something you wish to say to me, Lord Chilsten? Or do you merely intend to leave and go about your business until again I find myself on an outing with another gentleman whom you do not approve of and will therefore make it known to me?"

Cyrus took a deep breath. A mistake, for the scent of her

lilies embedded themselves further in his mind, leaving him wanting more. "I do not mean to stand in your way."

"No?" She laughed, pulling her hand away. "You punched Lord Perry in the face this evening. If that is not standing in my way, I do not know what is." She turned her head to the side, studying him as if he were some oddity. "Admit the truth to yourself if you will not admit it to me."

"And what truth is that?" he whispered, his attention shifting to her lips that were a little blue from the cold. Even so, he longed to taste them, kiss them until they were warm. She was so sweet, kind, and passionate, everything he did not require in a wife but everything his body and soul craved.

"That you're jealous of the men courting me. That deep down in that cloaked heart of yours, you have feelings for a woman of no rank who hails from a town so insignificant to the *ton* that I'm sure none of them know where it is. That you desire a woman who's more at home alone in the country with her horses and her dogs than in the *ton's* ballrooms. That you ought to ask me to be your wife properly this time and not on the side of a road, if that is what you want, before another gentleman asks me instead, and I say yes."

A shiver stole down his spine at the truth of her words. He stared at her, marveling at her beauty and ability to see through his visage. To know what he wanted deep inside his soul. A scary and liberating fact.

"There are things you do not know about me, Julia."

She chuckled, waving her hand and dismissing his words. "I know all there is to know about you, Lord Chilsten. You do not scare or intimidate me. However, you do," she said, running a finger down his waistcoat, poking him in the heart, "intrigue me and infuriate me with your stubbornness. I think we would suit better than you know."

Did that mean she would agree to be his wife? He stared at her, knowing he wanted her to be his. After tonight at the fear that ran through him at the thought of Lord Perry having used the day's unforeseen drama to his advantage and making her marry him instead, he knew that would never do.

He could not watch the woman before him marry another. She made his heart race, his body yearn. He could not have that reaction to her while she was married to someone else. He knew what would happen then. He would push for a clandestine affair, and he would gain one.

But it would not be enough.

He would not want to let her go once he had her.

"Will you marry me, Miss Julia Woodville?" he asked, taking her hands, feeling the chill of her fingers through her gloves. He ran his hands over hers, trying to warm them. "Be my wife and future marchioness?"

She started at his words. Clearly, she did not think her prodding at him would end the conversation with a proposal, but she was right. He could not watch her walk down the aisle with anyone else but him. He knew he had not told her everything, but he would as soon as they were married and their lives were joined forever. She would, in time, forgive him his mistake, and she would grow to love his child as much as he did. Julia was a caring soul. She would not hate him forever.

He hoped.

"You wish to marry me in truth?" she asked, not believing his words.

He nodded. "Yes, that is what I'm asking. I should not have blurted it on the road earlier tonight, but I want you to marry me. To become my wife." He glanced down at their linked hands, unable to hold her eye. "You are right, I cannot sit by and watch you marry anyone else, and therefore as a gentleman, I must ask for your hand for you to be mine and no one else's."

"I promised myself that I would not marry any man unless I loved him as much as he loved me. I will not break my oath."

"I think after today, that wish may be impossible. Suppose Lord Perry uses your being with him after dark and alone to force a union. In that case, you may find yourself betrothed to his lordship instead," he lied, knowing he would never allow Perry to use the situation to his advantage. But nor could he profess love as she wished, not when he was still unsure the emotions rioting inside of him were indeed that sentiment.

"I know that you were not in truth with him alone, but no one can prove otherwise, and I cannot allow any shadow to besmirch your name."

He cared for her too much for that. Was that not enough to make a happy and fulfilled marriage? He certainly hoped it was.

She stared at their hands, her brow furrowed in thought. "I cannot allow my family to suffer for my actions today, even though they were not my fault. If there is any inkling of a scandal, it may jeopardize my sisters, who are yet to debut." She sighed, and he loathed that she seemed dejected about his offer.

"I will be faithful, Julia. I promise to be the best husband I can be for you," he said, needing her to know that he would try to make her happy. Try to make their marriage the best it could be. She was not what he had thought he needed for a wife, but she was certainly what he wanted. And that overrode all other considerations.

"Very well," she nodded, meeting his gaze. "I will marry you, Lord Chilsten."

He smiled, a weight he did not know was pressing on his shoulders lifted. He would have thought the opposite would have occurred. It was odd that it did not.

CHAPTER
SIXTEEN

By the third week of the banns being called, Julia welcomed her mama and father to town and her younger sister Ashley, who was set to debut the next year. Her friend Reign had returned to Grafton two weeks before, but promised to attend the wedding.

Julia knew she had been so busy of late that she had missed seeing her friend at several events, but she could not help but wonder if Reign had returned home because the Marquess of Lupton-Gage had announced his betrothal to Lady Sally, Lord Perry's younger sister. An announcement met with surprise and much disappointment on her friend's behalf. If Julia knew her friend at all, she understood her to be heartbroken.

She sat under the shade of a willow tree in the gardens of the ducal London home and reveled in being alone for a moment. It was peaceful here, and thankfully someone had placed a wooden seat under the tree for those wishing to hide.

Only the slightest breeze dared sway the branches, and

birdsong completed the tranquil scene. If only her life were as peaceful. The fittings for her wedding gown had taken up much of the last few weeks, and now her mama was busy preparing her belongings and a new wardrobe to be shipped over to the Marquess of Chilsten's home upon their marriage.

She stared up at the green canopy, thinking of what life would be like married to Cyrus, how it would be to be with him each night and kiss and hold him whenever she wanted.

Butterflies took flight in her stomach. She wanted this last week to be over already so she could be the next Marchioness of Chilsten.

He did not declare his love, Julia.

She pursed her lips. In time, when they were married and living together, when they started their family, love would come. She was certain of it. His heart could not remain aloof and untouched forever. Not if she kept chipping away at it. He had already stated he would be faithful, which was a tremendous step forward for the rake he was.

"There you are. I was informed you were in the gardens, but I could not find you."

Julia's heart jumped at the sound of Lord Chilsten's voice. He pushed the willow branches aside and stepped into her cloaked, leafy world. She inwardly sighed at the sight of him. So tall, his broad shoulders making the little space beneath the tree seem even smaller. Her hands itched to touch him, remind herself that he was hers and no dowager duchess could come between them.

"The house is busy, and I needed time alone," she said, moving to the side of the chair so he could sit. "But you're welcome, of course."

He smiled, and her stomach twisted into delicious knots. The man had a way of unsettling her, and today was no different. Since the announcement of their betrothal, they had hardly been alone, and all she had wanted was such.

To be able to talk to him, settle the nerves that plagued her that he somehow regretted his offer. That he would be all that she hoped for in a husband, and what her marriage would become.

"I'm glad to hear it." He leaned down, stealing a kiss.

Julia leaned into him, not knowing how much she needed him to touch her, to reassure and comfort her. The knowledge that he did not love her plagued her still.

Julia slipped her hand about his neck, playing with the hair at his nape. "Are you certain this is what you want, my lord? It is forever, need I remind you."

He watched her a moment before scooping her off the seat and placing her on his lap. He clasped her cheeks in his hands, making her meet his eyes. "I would not have offered if I did not want you as my wife, my marchioness. I am many things, as you well know, but I am not a man who does not know his own mind. And my mind was made up the moment I thought of you married to anyone else but me."

"Very sweet words indeed. If I did not know you better, I might even believe what you are saying," she said, trying to lighten the mood. And yet her words were not far from the truth. He was a rake, renowned for his different lovers and scandals. His biggest so far, his hasty marriage the year before to a Scottish lady no one knew. And now here he was, engaged again...

"You wound me." He chuckled, his hand slipping along her thigh. Goosebumps rose on her skin at his touch. One more week and they would be wed, and he could touch and kiss her as much as she longed for him to do whenever he pleased.

His eyes darkened, flashed with heat, and her breath hitched. "What are you doing?" she asked him. Her gown bunched in his hand as he worked it up over her leg, exposing her silk stocking.

"You have such long legs. They ought to be seen more, do you not think?" he asked, his wicked grin leaving her with little doubt about what he had in mind.

"You cannot do anything here and now. We're in the garden, and anyone could come upon us."

He shrugged, his long, warm fingers slipping between her legs. She gasped, opened for him without protest, and cursed herself for the wanton she was when in his arms. "I want you, have thought of nothing but when we could be alone," he whispered, kissing her neck.

She pushed at him, attempting to stand, and he pulled her back onto his lap. "But that is the point, my lord. We're not alone. We're in my sister's garden, and my parents are here. You cannot seduce me under the willow tree."

His mouth pursed. "Where can I seduce you then? I cannot wait until our marriage to have you."

Julia shook her head, attempting to dislodge herself and gain her freedom. "No, I will not allow that. I have already given too many liberties, and should anything stop our wedding from going ahead... I do not want to be compromised." She leaned close to ensure privacy. "What if I was to get with a child?" she asked him. Did he not think of these things? Were his rakish wiles so reckless that he did not care? She could only hope what he said was true, and once they were married, he would be faithful.

"Nothing will stop me from marrying you, Julia. Nothing," he said again, his determined gaze soothing a little of the nerves that would not abate.

The canopy of the tree was pushed aside, and her sister Hailey stepped beneath the shade. She raised her brow at Chilsten, who merely stared back as if butter would not melt in his wickedly hot mouth.

"Chilsten, you ought not to be ensconced in here with my sister. *Alone*," she accentuated. "And in any case, you're wanted in the library. Father and Derby wish to discuss the marriage contracts."

Julia watched as he gained his feet and before her sister, and without a care, he dipped his head and kissed her. Julia did not move for fear of breaking the spell that he weaved about her. He grinned down at her, sensing her shock, before taking his leave.

Julia met Hailey's amused eyes and was glad that she was not angry. "Chilsten certainly seems smitten with you," her sister said, taking her hands in hers. "Your marriage will be a happy one, I believe."

Julia nodded, hoping that was true. "He does not love me as the duke loved you before your marriage. Or how much Viscount Leigh loves Isla. What if the deceased Lady Chilsten was the love of his life? Shall hold his heart for all time?"

Hailey entwined their arms as they walked back toward the house across the lawns. "Have you not seen how Chilsten looks at you, Julia? He may not have said he loves you, but I have little doubt that he does. I just do not think he knows the emotion yet to voice it."

A portion of hope flickered to life inside her. She had caught him at times watching her, his gaze wistful and amused. But was that love or only lust? "I wanted to know my husband loved me before any promises were made. But after Lord Perry's bungled outing, I suppose I shall not have that indulgence."

"No, you will not, but I do not hold any fears that your life will not be a happy and most enjoyable one with Chilsten. Is it not said that rakes make the best husbands?"

"I do not know. Mayhap you ought to tell me. Did not Derby have a little reputation prior to your marriage?" Julia teased.

Hailey chuckled, a light blush stealing over her cheeks. "I will tell you this, my darling sister. You will be happy. There is nothing that we do not know about Chilsten to sully your union. All will be well, and he will care for and love you just as you deserve. I would not have allowed the union to go ahead if I did not think that was the case. No matter the scandal that Lord Perry may have tried to stir."

Julia hugged her sister's arm, so happy that she had someone she could tell her worries to and know that she would never steer her in the wrong direction or give her false hope. Hailey was honest and forthright always.

"Shall we have some tea since the gentlemen are having something stronger? I know Ashley was desperate to discuss next year's Season plans. Are you sponsoring her?" Julia asked her.

"I can, of course, but you may if you like. By then, you will be the Marchioness of Chilsten, but I'm happy with whatever you decide."

They entered the drawing room and found their mama and Ashley seated together, pouring over the latest *Le Belle Assemblée*. Ashley, dark-haired like most of her sisters, had not gained Julia's height, but that did not matter. She had always reminded Julia of an angel, both due to her light, perfect complexion, and kindness. She would do well next year, and Julia could not wait to see how her Season played out.

"Sister!" Ashley said, jumping up and hugging her. "I'm so happy to be here, and I cannot wait for this evening. Are you certain it shall be appropriate for me to attend Lord and Lady Jenkin's ball? I'm not yet out."

Hailey nodded, seating herself beside their mama. "I'm the Duchess of Derby, and I'm escorting you. It will be perfectly fine."

Julia hugged Ashley back, happy to see one of her siblings since she missed the others still at home. They spoke of the latest on dit going about Grafton, mainly Mr. Bagshaw and his wife, one of the least-liked women in the county, and how they had put most of the small town offside by her manners and interference in everyone's lives.

"I shall wear my mauve gown this evening, Julia. What do you think?" Ashley asked her, smiling.

"I think that would be lovely."

"You should wear the new gown the modiste delivered earlier, Julia. It's such a pretty gold and will make your eyes shine," Ashley said.

Was her gown here? She had ordered it several weeks ago and was pleased that it was. Now that the news of her betrothal was about London, tonight was the first ball they would attend since that announcement and was sure to create a stir and much talk.

"I think you are right. I will wear my new gown." Now that she was to be the Marchioness of Chilsten, she would not have to put up with snide looks from the Dowager Duchess of Barker. Or have to suffer through more conversations with Lord Payne or Lord Perry, who had not even sent a note apologizing for his bungled excursion to the castle ruins.

Tonight was the start of forever with Cyrus, and she would enjoy every moment of it.

SEVENTEEN

The evening at Lord and Lady Jenkin's ball was like most *ton* events. The room was full to the brim with guests. Hundreds of candles lit the room, leaving a little wax on the floor and gowns whenever they dripped. The terrace doors were open, along with the windows, to quell the room's heat, which was already stifling.

Her gown of gold silk felt like a second skin. Her modiste had outdone herself with the dress. With her sister's yellow diamonds borrowed for the evening, she looked the part of the future Marchioness of Chilsten, of one of England's and Scotland's most prominent and influential families.

They made their way through the throng of guests, many stopping her sisters, the duchess, and viscountess to speak to them and offer Julia congratulations. She glanced at Ashley, who looked stunned and overwhelmed, but excited too. Julia also did not miss the interested glances from several gentlemen who noted the younger Woodville sister new to town.

A warm, strong hand settled on her back, and without turning, she knew who held her. "You're here, my lord?"

His warm breath tickled her neck, and she kept her attention on the guests, not needing anyone to know how much Chilsten's touch or words affected her. The man himself did not know what he made her feel, and she certainly did not want the *ton* to learn the truth about how much she was under the rake's spell.

"It's our unofficial betrothal ball. How could I not be here with you?" A small smile played about his wicked mouth, his eyes dipping to her gown, slipping over her like a physical caress. She shivered. "You look beautiful, Julia." He picked up her hand, kissing her gloved fingers. "I do not think I have ever been so taken aback by your beauty as I was tonight seeing you enter the room."

She met his eyes, seeing the truth of his words, and warmth spread through her. He thought she was beautiful. She had taken his breath away? Could she steal his heart too?

"You are very handsome yourself," she replied, not letting go of his hand and holding it at her side instead. His fingers tightened on hers, seemingly content to keep hold of her too. "Will you dance with me?" she asked him, and the notes of a country dance started to play.

"Always," he said, leading them onto the floor. He pulled her into his arms just as the dance commenced, other couples milling about them, cocooning them within their world.

"How am I to survive the next week without touching you, kissing you as much as I want to?" His eyes darkened at his words, dipping to her lips, which she had the over-whelming urge to lick.

"Tell me, my lord. If we were alone, right at this minute,

what would you do?" she asked, curious to know how rakish he would be with her should she allow it. Which a lot of the times she had already.

He spun her about, bringing her back into his arms. "First, I would kiss you, bring you to a feverish pitch from my kiss only." His gaze dipped once more to her mouth. "Your lips have always fascinated me. Full and so soft that one never wants to part from tasting them."

Nerves skittered across her skin, but she wanted to hear more. "And what else?" she asked, waiting for the dance to bring them back together again.

"I would touch you, bring your blood to boiling at my touch. This gown," he said, his hand flexing against her waist, "I would strip from your body, but not quickly, mind you. I would take my time, expose you to my inspection with the duty and care you deserve before I would do wicked things to you."

"Similar to what we have done already?" she asked him.

He growled, his eyes darkening further. "Oh yes, but I would not end our night with my mouth. I would have you in all ways and every way I can." He closed his eyes a moment, a pained expression on his face. "You make me want to steal you away now. I cannot wait for us to be married."

Julia could not either, and she hoped the emotions that stormed through him meant that more could come from their marriage. To make him feel as much as she feared she did already for the man in her arms.

She cared for him, wanted to hear his opinion, and have him respect hers. She wanted to make him content, for their time to be happy and pleasurable. She wanted him to love her as much as she loved him.

"I, too, wish that we were married, my lord. I want to be

alone with you just as much. I hope you believe that of me, no matter how our betrothal came about or our initial friendship."

"You mean when you kissed me at your sister's ball last Season because you wished to learn?" He chuckled. "I should have known that our lives would become entangled from there. Your heart is as wicked as mine."

She grinned, not doubting that as truth. "One week, and you will be mine. Are we to remain in town, or will we travel to your estate in Sussex?"

"We shall travel to our country estate a few days after our wedding. I want to be alone with you for a time. Have you all to myself."

She laughed just as the dance came to a reluctant end. He walked her back to where her sisters stood and she introduced him to her younger sister Ashley before he offered to dance with her sibling, who, beyond excited, accepted before being swept out onto the dance floor.

Julia laughed but found her amusement soon waned at the sight of the Dowager Duchess of Barker sauntering toward her. Her posse of hateful friends following in her wake.

"Miss Julia, my congratulations on your betrothal. I must admit I was surprised that the marquess asked for your hand in marriage. I did not think his lordship was interested in being married again. Not to an untitled country mouse in any case."

Julia pasted on a smile she hoped would not slip. She did not want the dowager to know how much she loathed her or her nasty mannerisms toward herself and other debutantes making their debut this year. She had been spiteful all Season and her confronting her now was merely to be mean.

"Thank you. I shall pass on your felicitations to his lordship when he returns."

She waved her words aside, scoffing. "Do not bother, my dear. I shall tell Chilsten myself when we're next alone. We are old friends, as you know."

Julia nodded once. "Of course. Whatever you prefer," she answered, not wanting to cause any further animosity than there already was, even though her words sent a spike of fear through her. Would they be alone later? Surely the dowager duchess was merely putting her on her guard and making her worry over nothing.

"It is a shame about his first wife, is it not? What large slippers you have to fill being the next Marchioness of Chilsten. I heard that the late marchioness was a great beauty and loved by her staff and tenants in England and Scotland. She will be sadly missed."

Julia narrowed her eyes, her hold on her emotions slipping. "You knew the marchioness then?" she asked, having thought not many did know the lady in the society. The late marchioness had not left Scotland as far as she had been told. Had she been wrong about that too?

The duchess laughed, a high-pitched sound that made her teeth clench. "Oh, no, I was not so fortunate. Rumor has it the marquess did not care to have her out of his sight, and they were nestled most of their time in Scotland." The duchess smirked. "I should think they kept each other pleasantly occupied," she said, her intention not missed by Julia.

"I'm sad for the marquess then for losing a woman he loved so very dearly." Julia raised her chin, refusing to allow the emotions that ran high within her to reveal themselves. Especially in front of the dowager duchess.

She swallowed the lump in her throat and blinked,

thinking of anything but the idea that she was marrying a man who had not stated that he loved her at all and yet seemed to have had a happy and loving marriage already.

Was the duchess trying to tell her to be on guard with the marquess? To guard her heart against the pain and disappointment that was sure to come?

Julia looked out over the throng of guests and could see Cyrus speaking to her mama and sister Ashley after their dance.

In truth, she knew very little about him. He had never spoken of his wife or their life together. Was it because he found the topic painful? She hoped she could help heal his pain and be his next grand love, but what if she never was? What if he never proclaimed to love her as she wished?

"Do not look so downcast, my dear," the dowager duchess said. "You're to be married in a few days, and you will be the new Marchioness of Chilsten. I'm certain with your background being a farmer's daughter, your tenants and staff will find common interests in you, and you too will be much loved."

"My father is a gentleman, Your Grace. We own land, yes, but we do not work it ourselves, just as I'm certain you have never toiled on your family's lands." Julia would listen to and allow certain words to move about her and not become embedded under her skin, but she would not permit a slight against her parents to go unchallenged.

"Of course, my dear," she said, sarcasm dripping from her words like poison. "I meant no offense. I hope you did not take any to our conversation. I was merely trying to guide you a little before you're a married woman and running one of the largest estates in England."

Julia threw her a small smile, but what she really wanted to do was give the woman and her smirking friends at her side the cut direct. Of course, she meant to insult her and make her uneasy over her forthcoming marriage—a fact she did not need any further help with since she was already anxious.

"Thank you for your consideration of me, but I assure you, as a woman who has a duchess and viscountess as sisters, I'm more than cared for and guided in this society." Julia dipped into a curtsy and left, needing to be away from them. That this life, these women would be part of her existence as the new marchioness left a sour taste in her mouth. But she would not rise to their poking. She would walk away, just as she had done so this evening.

Julia took a deep breath, trying to settle the nerves that threatened to overwhelm her. Her marriage to the marquess would succeed. He would come to love her. She was sure of it. They merely needed time. It may not be how she wanted to start her married life, but he was a kind, thoughtful, and handsome man who made her want things no well-bred young lady ought. Their start would be better than others in her social sphere. Eventually, they would be incandescently happy. They had to be.

CHAPTER
EIGHTEEN

Cyrus stood at the top of the church altar, cooling his heels as he waited for his bride, who was already ten minutes late. He glanced back at Derby, his witness, who threw him a small, comforting smile. It did not make the nerves that skittered across his skin lessen. Was she going to come? Was the whole *ton* about to watch him be stood up on his wedding day? What a blow to a renowned rake and what, in truth, he deserved. Marrying Julia with so much of his life hidden from her was not what he ought to have done. He should have told her the truth and allowed her to choose her future.

The doors to the church opened, and the weight he did not know he was carrying lifted from his shoulders. A violinist started to play, and he watched, enthralled at the sight of Julia walking toward him, her father holding her hand securely on his arm.

Soon, she would be his, and nothing could tear her from his side, not his past nor anything else. He swallowed the lump in his throat as he took her in. Her gown of light blue silk, trimmed with silver stitching, made her appear ethereal and timeless. She wore the Duke of Rothes's diamonds that he had sent for from Scotland, knowing she did not have any jewelry of her own.

She sparkled like the diamonds she wore, perfect and flawless. Something in his chest thumped hard, and he rubbed his hand over his waistcoat, trying to ease the pain. Her father kissed her cheek and whispered something in her ear that made her eyes sparkle before passing her over to him.

Cyrus took her hand, determined never to let it go. "You look beautiful, Julia," he said, meaning every word. He took a deep breath and fought not to allow the emotions that rallied inside him to gain control. He swallowed repeatedly, and he thought there might be something wrong with him for a moment.

She smiled up at him, her mouth alluring as always. Guilt prickled down his spine that he was marrying her, and she did not know all she should of his life. Of the life she was stepping into.

Of wife and mother. Not that he thought she would not forgive him for his child. Babies did occur naturally after marriage, but he had not told her of his daughter. Or how it came about that he had married the child's mother.

Rogue he may be, but he would not propagate his seed about England and not face the consequences of those actions like his father had done. But would his beautiful, sweet Julia forgive him? Would she hate him knowing he married her while keeping such a large truth from her?

"Repeat after me," he heard the reverend state.

They both followed directions, answering and relaying what the reverend said when required, and soon a bellow of cheers and clapping sounded, and they were married.

Not willing to wait for them to be alone, Cyrus pulled

Julia against him and kissed her. She did not shy away from his touch, and he knew she was the perfect match to his soul—the other half of his being.

The new Marchioness of Chilsten.

His wife.

He pulled back, staring down at her, marveling at her passion and beauty, her kindness and good heart. "Happy?" he asked her—the emotions of pleasure, satisfaction, and contentment thrumming through him like wine.

"So happy," she answered. "And you?" she asked in return.

"The same," he said, the words not merely enough to convey how he felt right at this moment. As if his heart was too full of happiness that it could burst. "So happy you are mine." Finally.

The wedding breakfast was held at her new home and the Marquess of +Chilsten's London town house. All of London was there, and for several hours they mingled and thanked those who had attended their wedding.

For the hundredth time since the reverend pronounced them husband and wife, Cyrus leaned down, stealing a kiss. His hand had not left her waist, and she could not help but smile each time his fingers flexed against her waist or the slight shift that brought her closer to him.

"Tell me again how much longer we must endure this breakfast before I can send everyone away and have you all to myself?" he asked again, his lips thinning into a displeased line. "It is past luncheon. Should they not be gone by now?"

She chuckled, sipping her wine. Each time she looked at him, when their eyes met, the pit of her stomach flipped and made her ache for what was to come. No longer did they need to steal time to be together. Now she could kiss and touch her husband as much as she liked. And she liked it a lot.

"Soon, I believe, but you know, husband, that we can merely slip away. We do not need to be here to allow our guests to continue celebrating."

He met her eyes, a devilish light sparkling in his. "Has my wickedness been a bad influence on you, Julia? I do believe it has been."

She reached out, fisting his waistcoat into her hand. "You are not the only one who wants, my lord. Do you not see?" she asked him.

His nose flared, his hand flexing on her hip before dipping low across her back. "Shall we excuse ourselves then, my dear? I do believe it is time."

Julia slipped out of his hold and started for the house without a word. Expectation thrummed through her at the possibility of what they were about to do. Finally, she would be with him as she had wanted for so long. She did not care that her guests would be left wondering where they were. Let them gossip and assume, they were married now and were doing nothing wrong.

Cyrus clasped her hand upon making the house, and they ran through the drawing room, into the foyer, and up the stairs. Julia laughed at the startled glances of their staff as they made their way to their suite of rooms.

Cyrus pulled her into his chamber, shutting and locking the door behind him. The breath in Julia's lungs seized at the sight he made. So virile and muscular, his chest rising and falling with each breath. His hair was slightly mussed from their exertion, leaving him disheveled and wild.

Julia walked up to him, running her hands through his

dark locks, pushing the few wayward curls from his face. She wanted to see him. All of his handsomeness. Everything that she loved so much more than she thought possible.

Without words, she reached behind herself and started to unhook her gown. Cyrus watched her all but a moment before he stripped himself of his clothes. His jacket and waistcoat fell to the floor, and with trepidation, she watched as he lifted his shirt over his head.

Her mouth dried, and she bit her lip as his tanned, muscular stomach came into view. She had never seen him so naked. He reached for the falls of his breeches, and Julia could not tear her gaze from his person. With a slowness that bordered on glacier speed, he flicked open the buttons, revealing himself to her.

He pushed down his breeches, kicked off his boots, and stood before her naked and proud. She felt her mouth gape at the sight of him. His size! Would they even fit? Would being with him hurt?

He turned her about, kissing her neck as he stripped her of her gown. So distracted by his touch on her body, she had only managed to untie a few hooks. He faced her again and kneeled, lifting her leg and gifting her a wicked grin, before slipping one then the other silk stocking from her legs, kissing her skin and leaving heat in his mouth's wake.

And then she was in his arms, carried with determined strides to his bed. They fell onto the cushioned mattress, legs tangled, kisses reigning supreme. He tasted of sin and sweet wine, and she drank from him, taking her fill.

He settled between her legs, and she could feel his hardness against her aching, wet flesh.

"Do not be afraid, Julia darling. It will only hurt but a moment. I promise to make this wonderful for you."

His mouth crushed down on hers, and she moaned,

clasping his locks and kissing him back with the desire and need that burned between them.

"You're so beautiful. So wonderful," he murmured, reaching down and lifting her legs to settle about his hips. Julia took a calming breath, having never felt so exposed as she did now, but his kisses, his sweet words, soothed the anxiety that rose at the thought of making love to him for the first time.

She had never done such a thing before. What if he found her lacking? Boring even? She shuddered at the thought.

"Kiss me," she begged, needing him to distract her, even from her own thoughts.

Cyrus needed no further urging. He covered her lips with his, drinking from her as he adjusted himself to be with her finally. He slowly pushed into her with as much care as he could summon. The sensation that this was where they were supposed to be rushed through him and made him dizzy with pleasure.

Julia stilled beneath him as he settled deep within her. He was motionless a moment, not wanting to hurt her more than he may have already. He was not a small man, and she was a virgin. He needed to remind his wicked tendencies of that. In time they could do more, but tonight was not that time.

She threw her head back, and he kissed her neck, lathing her skin with her tongue. She lifted her legs, undulating on him and his mind reeled. "I... Are you going to move?" she asked.

He chuckled, taking the opportunity to dip his head and

kiss her breasts. "You want me to move?" He pulled out, thrusting in again.

She gasped, her eyes fluttering closed in desire. "Yes. Like that."

Certain that she was comfortable and relaxed, Cyrus thrust deeper this time, eliciting a moan. He increased his pace, enjoying the wonder, the pleasure that settled on her features. He wanted to please her, make this day the most wonderful, most memorable of her life.

Her hands skittered down his back, her nails scoring his skin. Desire, want, and need coursing through him. She pushed against him with her mons, seeking him deeper, harder. He gave her what she wanted, forgetting that this was her first time and fucking her as she liked.

Hard.

Swift.

He reached down, holding one ass cheek and tipping her pelvis. The action was a trick he had learned and one that he always knew made the woman reach her pinnacle without issue.

Julia was no different. Her wide eyes met his as he continued to taunt and tease her to distraction.

"Cyrus," she gasped, bucking and rolling her hips to help her gain what she wanted. Julia pushed at his chest, tipping him off balance, and he was on his back. She came above him, positioning herself on his cock and the breath in his lungs seized.

She was a goddess, a woman who knew what she wanted and would take it without question or guilt. How he adored her so.

She fucked him without restraint. He watched her, enthralled, having never expected such a thing from her. Not yet, at least. Her hair fell in waves over her breasts. Her cheeks flushed, her lips swollen and red from their many kisses.

He fought for control, to remain calm and not spend before she had reached her peak. She took him, threw her head back, rode him, and used him for her pleasure. The rake in him growled with satisfaction, loving that his wife was so spirited.

His balls tightened, and he breathed deep and fought to hold on to his self-control hanging by a thread. He clasped her hips, thrusting hard and fast. Her fingers settled on his chest. Sweat pooled on their skin, the scent of sex, desire, and jasmine intoxicated the air.

"Cyrus," she gasped.

He thrust hard, once, twice, taking her as she wished. She cried out, her breasts rocking as she climaxed. Her core spasmed around his cock and drew his release forward with such speed that his head spun.

"Julia," he cried out, his mind in a whirl, breathless and without sense. The words he had never uttered to anyone sat on the edge of his lips but did not fall. Cyrus stared up at her as she enjoyed the last of her pleasure.

Realization ran through him at what he had almost said.

I love you...

Another complication to add to his long list.

NINETEEN

J ulia woke late the next day, her body rested and content. She felt like she was living a dream that she did not want to end. Their first night as husband and wife was one she would not forget, and cherish forever.

"His lordship sent up a bath for you, my lady," her maid said, placing a cup of tea beside her bed along with a piece of toast, her staple breakfast.

"Thank you, Masie, that sounds lovely," she said.

Julia lounged in bed for a time, enjoyed her breakfast before soaking in the tub, and used the lily soap before her maid helped her dress in a morning gown of blue muslin. She wrapped a shawl about her shoulders as the morning turned chill, and the distinct smell of rain floated in the air.

She started downstairs, wanting to see Cyrus. To be near him, read a book while he worked, or if she could convince him, seduce him back upstairs so he could show her more of what pleasure could be had now that they were a married couple.

The sound of a woman's hurried voice slowed her steps

in the foyer, and she halted outside the library door that sat ajar. Although the occupants inside the room could not see her, she could hear them without fault, and their words sent a chill through her heart.

"What are you doing here?" Cyrus asked the unknown woman. "I informed you to travel directly to my Sussex estate, not my London home. You must leave. Now, before anyone sees you."

The pit of Julia's stomach twisted into a knot, and she clasped her stomach, unsure what they were talking about but not liking Cyrus's tone or the profuse apologies that tumbled from the woman's lips.

"My apologies, my lord. I must have read the missive wrong," the woman said. Julia frowned as the sound of a child cooing and trying to speak joined in the conversation with Cyrus and his guest.

The woman shushed the babe, keeping it soothed. "We shall leave right away. I hope I have not caused any trouble for you, my lord. That was not my intention. I made a mistake, and it will not happen again."

"All will be well," Cyrus said. "The house is not yet up, and no harm done. I merely wanted to discuss this matter with my wife at Chapleigh House, not here in London. If you could take Freya to Chapleigh, I shall join you in a week or two."

"Very good, my lord." There was a pause before the woman continued, "Shall I take Freya from you now, my lord? I shall leave immediately."

"Of course," he said.

Julia had heard enough. She pushed the door open, entered the library, and met the startled gaze of her husband and the elderly, unknown woman who spoke to him. But even more odd was the vision of her husband handing over a small child, a year old, if she could hazard a guess. A little girl with the prettiest golden locks with a touch of red weaving through them looked at her and smiled. Julia had seen that smile before...

"My lord," she said, moving closer and studying the little girl named Freya. She was a sweet-faced little cherub, but who she was and why she was here was a mystery. That her husband, the marquess, was holding the said babe too did not make any sense. "Introduce me to your guests," she said, trying to remain polite and not be seized with panic.

Something about the fear that sparked in Cyrus's eyes gave her little comfort, and she steeled herself for what was to come.

"Julia, darling, this is Mrs. McCallum and Freya. They were just leaving."

The woman took the child successfully this time from Chilsten, and leaned down, picking up a small, leather valise at her side. "It was lovely meeting you, Lady Chilsten," Mrs. McCallum stated with a small smile.

Julia managed a smile in return while studying the woman. A nanny, she presumed. The child certainly did not resemble the older woman at all. Which left Julia with the question of to whom the child belonged.

Before she could ask, the woman bustled out of the room as if the devil himself was nipping at her leather boots, and they were soon alone in the library, leaving Julia to wonder if she had imagined the woman and child in the room at all.

"You know Mrs. McCallum how, my lord? You have not mentioned them before. Are they related to you? A cousin, perhaps?" Julia asked, coming to sit on the chair before his desk. Cyrus rubbed a hand over his jaw, slumping into his chair opposite her and shuffling several missives about his desk.

He appeared nervous, and unease shivered down her spine.

She didn't say a word and waited as patiently as she could. Finally, Cyrus glanced up from his simulated business and met her eye. "I did not want to tell you so soon. I wanted us to spend some time together, learn more about each other before my past reared up and spooked you."

"Your past?" she asked. "What do you mean?"

He cringed, leaning back in his chair and watching her. His silence was unnerving.

"Cyrus, who was that woman and child?"

He closed his eyes but a moment before he said, "The woman is Mrs. McCallum, as introduced. She is the nanny to Lady Freya Chilsten. My daughter."

For a moment, Julia could do nothing but blink. His child? She glanced out the window, thinking over his words. They made no sense. His child? How could that be? Surely he would have told her. Was not the existence of a child something one told another before making them their wife?

"You had a child with your first wife? It bothers me that you didn't tell me such an important thing about you. Do you not think I ought to know that I'm to be a mother to a babe before we were married?"

"Of course you deserved to know, but that is not why I did not tell you. I had little concern over you taking on the child as your own, but there are circumstances of her birth that I worried you would not forgive."

"Such as?" Julia's mind raced with situations that could have occurred that stopped Cyrus from telling her the truth. Did he not trust her enough to be honest with her?

What was so bad about the child that would prevent her from taking on the responsibility? Julia relaxed her hands, realizing she was clasping the seat as if she were fearful of tumbling to the floor.

"I want to say that I never meant to hurt anyone. I made an error of judgment, and I hope you can find it in your heart to forgive me."

Julia raised her hand, halting his words. "Please just tell me, Cyrus. I'm starting to think the worst, and you're scaring me." And he was, awfully so.

"The child is from my marriage with my first wife. We found out she was increasing, and I fled to Scotland to marry her before the child was born. I did not shirk from my responsibility and would not allow any offspring of mine to be born out of wedlock."

Julia nodded. All of that sounded reasonable to her. "Who was the lady that you loved before? Was her family very angry at you both for what you had done?" Julia asked, trying to understand why he thought she would not take on his child. Or would not understand that he had a child with his first wife. What kind of person would she be who would disapprove of such a natural occurrence when one was married?

"She did not have any family, Julia." He frowned down at his hands on his desk, his fingers playing with a quill. "She was my maid."

The room spun at his words, and Julia stared at the man she married. Her husband now. Their marriage consummated, and there was no turning back. His maid? She swallowed. Hard.

"You slept with a woman who worked for you? Who was under your protection?" she asked, bile rising in her throat.

Did the man have no morals at all? Who would do such a thing? Her mind jumped from thought to thought. Images of all the maids they had working for them in this house. Had he slept with any of those? Did they know their master as well as Julia did? She sneered at the thought. Maybe they knew him better than she ever would, for she did not know the liar before her.

His servant? Dear God, he was the worst of men.

"The maid was of age, and the night it occurred was consensual, even though that plays a little part of it. She wrote to me, telling me of the impending child, and I refused to allow a child of mine to be born out of wedlock. I may have been a rake, a scoundrel even at times, but I have morals that would not let her face alone what we both had done. I fled to Scotland and married her, but she passed in childbirth."

A sad ending, to be sure, and not one that Julia could blame Cyrus for. But she could blame him for the lies he chose to tell and continued to say right up to their wedding. "I do not know who you are at all, do I? You pretended to be my friend, but a friend does not lie about such an important thing in their life. You ought to have told me of Freya."

"I was afraid you would not marry me. I realized that I could not stomach watching you marry anyone else, and therefore you and I were best suited."

"And why is that when you were determined only to marry a woman of rank at the beginning of our friendship?" Julia stopped her mind jumping from thought to thought. "I wasn't lofty enough to save you from this scandal that's about to ensue when this becomes known, was I? That is why you courted the Dowager Duchess of Barker, is it not? She is high enough in the peerage that any scandal or skeletons you have in your past can be swept aside by the rank you would hold over the *ton*.

"But with me, that is not the case. I'm gentry, not nobility. However will you survive such a fall from grace when this becomes known? For if one thing is crystal clear today, you care about what people think far more than you let on." She shook her head. The pain cutting her deep inside was unbearable. "I will be no help to you all. Us both and your daughter will be shamed and ostracised no matter what I do."

His eyes blazed across the desk, and she refused to look away. "I could not marry anyone else because somewhere during our friendship, I fell in love with you. I do not care what becomes of my name or what people think of me, so long as I have you by my side. I could not lose you."

Julia stared, astonished. "You love me?" She laughed, the idea of such a thing too comical to believe. "You do not. You do not love me at all. You're a liar who slept with their maid, just as you seduced me before marriage. I do not know why you offered for me at all. Mayhap you do not like the idea of me with anyone else, but love? No, you do not love me."

Julia stood and strode to the window. She pushed back the heavy velvet curtains and watched people at the park across the square. "You may have been jealous. I will grant you that emotion, but not love." She turned and met his eye, forcing the lump in her throat to subside. "I have never lied to you or kept any truths that I thought you should know before our marriage. That is love, Cyrus. Not what you have done and kept from me. That is not love."

Julia strode from the room, meeting her maid upstairs as she was bringing fresh linens into her room. "Please pack my things. I'm leaving," she ordered.

Her maid gaped before dipping into a curtsy and following her into the room. "Do you wish for me to pack much, my lady? Or an overnight bag? What would you prefer?" she asked.

"Pack most of my things. We're leaving for the Chilsten estate in Sussex as soon as a carriage can be hitched. Please have that prepared too if you will." She had a child to meet properly and care for, and she would be damned if she would allow her husband to let the child go parentless another moment longer. The little girl was innocent in all of this mess. She would not allow her to suffer any further for it.

She shook her head, thinking of the small child of twelve months of age who did not know who her parents were or if anyone loved her. A terrible notion that she would not allow to continue a moment longer.

She was the Marchioness of Chilsten now, and through marriage, she was the child's mother from this day forward, and she would be damned if she would falter in this responsibility. She would revel in it, and the child would thrive because of her care and love.

And Lord Chilsten could go to the devil for his duplicity if she did not first send him there herself.

CHAPTER
TWENTY

Cyrus did not see Julia for the remainder of the day. He hoped keeping his distance from her would help calm her a little after their argument several hours before. He finished his dinner in the dining room alone, ignoring the knowing looks from his servants who waited on him.

Tonight they were supposed to attend the Mason's ball, but looking at the time, he did not think that now likely.

He went upstairs, determined to speak to her, to explain better perhaps what had happened between himself and his maid. Not that he could explain much. He had acted like a cad when the opportunity arose and created a child from that error.

He would not be the first gentleman to have had such a situation transpire, and he doubted he would be the last, but it was not the child or even so much that it had been a maid he had married that upset Julia, but that he had lied about it. If only he could explain why he had married her, maybe she would forgive him.

But still, he had kept important information from her,

not allowing her to decide if he were the type of man she wanted to marry. The image he had portrayed to her held untruths, smoke, and mirrors, and he did not know if she would ever forgive him for those deceptions.

Making the upstairs landing, he looked in on his suite of rooms and found it empty, but for the small fire burning in its grate and several candles lit for the evening.

Crossing the passage, he knocked on the marchioness's door and, hearing no reply, tried again. "Julia," he called out, hoping she would grant him entrance. They needed to speak, to try to find some path forward. "May I come in?" he asked, listening but hearing nothing.

"My lord?"

He turned to find the upstairs parlor maid watching him, a large jug of water in her hands.

"Are you looking for Lady Chilsten?" the maid asked him.

He nodded. "Yes, has she left for the Mason's ball already?" He supposed he could not blame her for being angry with him and leaving him behind. He was probably the last person she wanted to see right now. If only she gave him time, allowed him to explain.

"She is not here, my lord. This morning she ordered a carriage to be brought around."

"To travel where?" he asked, unable to hide the shock that ricocheted through him. Had she left him? Had she returned to her sister, the duchess's home? Or Grafton? Was their marriage over before it had even begun? He reached out, using the wall to steady himself, when his vision blurred.

His maid's eyes went wide, and he took a calming breath before he startled the servant any further.

"To your country estate, my lord. She had her maid pack

her things, and they left this morning in one of the family carriages for Chapleigh House." She glanced about, if unsure of herself. "Apologies, my lord. We thought you were aware."

He stormed to his room and rang for his valet. No, he was not aware. He had no idea she had fled London to travel to his country estate. Why had she done such a thing? His steps faltered when the realization struck. She had gone to his estate because that is where his daughter was headed. Did she wish to meet her or dismiss her from that house? He did not think the latter unless it was he that she dismissed from her life.

The notion did not bear thinking about. His valet entered the room. "You rang, my lord?"

"Pack up my things, Smithers. We're heading to Chapleigh first thing tomorrow morning. The marchioness is already on her way, and I wish to be hot on her heels if possible."

"Of course, my lord," Smithers said, moving toward his wardrobes and pulling out and assessing what he would pack. Cyrus watched him for a moment and then went to the decanter of whisky he kept in his room and poured himself a large dram.

She would forgive him for keeping his daughter a secret from her. In time she would understand why he had married his maid and not merely let her suffer the consequences of sleeping with a man who was not her husband or equal.

Julia had to forgive him, for he was not sure he could live if she loathed him forever. Not now when he loved her so dearly and wanted nothing but to be with her, love her, just as she deserved.

. . .

The carriage rolled to a stop before Chapleigh House. The magnificent square Georgian building looked to have hundreds of rooms and just as many servants. A line of footmen and maids stood outside the double doors, and she jumped down, glad that the butler came forward and introduced himself.

"Lady Chilsten, we hoped you would arrive, and we're very pleased to make your acquaintance." He gestured for her to enter, and she smiled at the staff as she made her way indoors. If the outside of the house had taken her breath away, the interior left her speechless.

Marble floors and a large, central spiraling staircase greeted her. The house was clean, and flowers sat on two ornate sideboards in the foyer, magnific family paintings hung on every wall.

"Your rooms are prepared and waiting for you upstairs. I shall have your maid unpack your things."

"Thank you," she said, following the butler, unable to stop taking in the unexpected gift that was the house. She knew that the family she had married into was powerful and wealthy, but this home appeared grander than her sister's, the duchess, in Kent. The responsibilities that she now held doubled in weight, not to mention the little girl she had to meet and raise, was also a surprise.

The thought of the little child brought forth a rush of maternal instincts and protection. She may not be noble or have been born a lady, but she was respectable and would not allow Lady Freya to be looked down upon, no matter how her birth came about.

Her room, which had an adjoining door to the marquess's, was spacious with its own dressing and bathing room. The floral silk wallpaper was pretty and reminded her of the natural beauty of the gardens back at Grafton. She did not think she would change them, so perfect did they suit her.

She strolled about the room, taking in her furniture, the daybed before the fire, and the small ladies' writing desk near the window.

"I hope everything is acceptable, my lady?" the butler asked, standing on the threshold.

"It is lovely, thank you." She paused, meeting his pleased gaze. "If you would send for Mrs. McCallum and Lady Freya, please. I want to speak to them in the parlor. If you would also show me where that is, that would be most welcome."

The butler bowed, gesturing for her to follow him. "If you come this way, my lady, I shall take you there directly and do as you ask."

Julia followed him down a long passageway to the opposite side of the house. He nodded toward an empty room with large, floor-to-ceiling windows that looked out onto the manicured grounds below.

"I shall return with Mrs. McCallum and Lady Freya, my lady. I will also have tea brought up for you. You must be parched after your long journey."

"Thank you," Julia said, strolling to the windows and looking out on the grounds. Had she not been so very angry at Cyrus, the house and gardens would have made her giddy with delight that all of this was now hers. But the cad had lied to her. Deceived her.

It was not so much that he had a child with his first wife but that he had broken the trust between employer and employee. Sleeping with a maid indeed. What had the man been thinking? The poor little girl, now motherless too, made the situation sadder still.

How could he have lied to me?

"Lady Chilsten?"

Julia turned to see the woman she had witnessed in Lord Chilsten's library two days past standing before her with a small child holding her hand at her side. "Good afternoon, Mrs. McCallum. I'm happy to make your acquaintance." Julia bobbed down, smiling at the little girl. "Hello, Freya. My name is Julia. It is lovely to meet you at last."

The older woman shuffled in her pocket and pulled out a handkerchief.

Julia looked up at her and saw that she was overcome with emotion. "You were worried I would not be kind to the child, were you not?" Coming over to the older woman, Julia said, "Come, sit with me, and we will talk. We have much to discuss."

The little girl looked up at Julia, and she held out her hands, hoping the child would come to her. Freya ran to her with a bright smile and reached to be picked up. Julia pulled her into her arms, staring at the little face so like her father's, and her heart missed a beat.

"You're a very sweet little cherub. I hope that we can be friends, and you'll allow me to be your mama." Not that Julia expected Freya to understand or comprehend her words, but she wanted her to know that from the very first, Freya was as much hers as she was Chilsten's child. And no one would think differently.

They sat on the settees before the fire, and Julia smiled as Freya played with the small doll she held in her hands. "As you know, I'm the Marchioness of Chilsten now, and as such, I'm Freya's stepmama. But I do not like that term, so I will be just her mama, if you will. I'm from a large and loving family, and I promise you, Mrs. McCallum, that I shall do all that I can to shield and love Freya as if she were born of my own flesh. I hope that you will stay on as her nanny since she seems quite fond and trusting of you, and her adjustment here may take time, and she'll be looking for people to trust."

The older woman sniffed, dabbing at her cheeks. "I cannot express how thankful I am to hear you say this, my lady. Lord Chilsten cares for the girl and loves her, but he returned to London, and we always knew that in time he would marry again. To have married a woman of such morals, with such a caring heart, well, it warms the cockles of my heart that you are the new marchioness."

Julia smiled, more than happy to be a mother for Freya. She wanted many children herself, and having Freya merely meant that wish came true sooner than later. Not that her happiness over meeting the child and caring for her in any way absolved Cyrus from the lies he told her. He would not be so easily forgiven.

"I am glad he's been a good father to her, and you need not worry any further about how I shall treat Freya. I could not live with myself if I blamed an innocent child for the happenings of her parents. I will care for and love her as my own. I promise you that."

A knock sounded on the door, and the butler entered, carrying a tray of tea and sandwiches. "It is past luncheon, but cook made up some repast for you, my lady. If you care to break your fast."

"Thank you," she said, reaching for a small sandwich and passing it to Freya, whose eyes sparkled at the sight of food. "Would you care for some yourself, Mrs. McCallum?" Julia asked, pouring them both tea. "There is more to discuss. We should probably settle in for a little tête-à-tête."

The older woman smiled, taking the cup of tea Julia handed her. "What else would you like to discuss, my lady? I'm more than happy to convey any information you wish. Or to discuss Lady Freya's schedule."

Julia leaned back on the settee, smiling as Freya lay down and placed her head in her lap, the half-eaten sandwich still clasped in her small, chubby hand.

"Tell me about Freya's mama. If she wishes to know of her later in life, I should know as much as I can about her. Let us start there," she said, settling back to learn all that she could of Chilsten's life before her that she knew nothing of.

A life he had kept hidden from her until now.

TWENTY-ONE

Cyrus arrived late at Chapleigh House and found only the footman awake in the foyer. He ordered the young lad to stay where he was, that he would require nothing for the evening, and made his way upstairs to his suite of rooms.

After bathing and dismissing his valet, he went to the adjoining door that led into the marchioness's rooms. He had not seen Julia for two days, and they had been the longest of his life. How had he gone so long without her being his wife?

He could not imagine her being anything but with him from this day forward if she would forgive him.

He knocked on the door but, hearing no reply, tried again before opening it a little. He glanced into the room and found Julia sitting in her bed, a candle flickering on the bedside table, the sheer shift she wore taunting him with its transparency.

Hoping it was safe and she would not throw the book that sat in her lap at his head, he slipped into the room, moving toward her with cautious steps.

"You left me," he blurted, having not meant to say those words at first but unable to take them back now that he had spoken them.

"Not without cause," she remarked, her tone chillier than the air outside. He sat on the end of the bed, guessing this was as safe a place as any.

"I'm sorry I did not tell you what happened last year. I was ashamed, and I panicked. I did not think that you would marry me, love me if you knew the truth of my life."

She crossed her arms over her chest. The action only accentuated her breasts further and taunted him over what he no longer could touch and kiss, love as he wanted.

"I probably would not have, not upon our first meeting, but surely you must have known that by me giving you liberties that I cared for you. I loved you, and still, you kept Freya a secret from me. Of how she came to be, and that was wrong, Cyrus." Julia shook her head, the disappointment in her brown eyes shaming him. "Tell me why you married the maid. Not that I do not think that is noble, but it is not the character of men such as yourself. Most gentlemen who get a child upon an innocent servant leave them to suffer their fate far away from their view. Explain to me what happened so that I may understand."

Cyrus sighed, rubbing a hand along his stubbled jaw. "My parents, both of them bedded many lovers throughout their lives and without shame or secret, even before me. My father's rakehell lifestyle, I suppose, rubbed off on me in many ways, except one. I swore I would never sire children all over England as he had done and leave them to their fate."

He stood, walking to the window and looking out over the grounds. "As it was, my own birth was almost illegitimate. If it were not for my mother's father forcing my father to the altar, none of this would be mine," he explained. "I have been so careful, even with my wayward ways, but when Freya's mama wrote and told me she was expecting, I could not leave her to face the consequences alone. I rode to Scotland and married her over the anvil without a second thought, and seven days later, Freya was born. You know the rest of the story from there."

Had you slept with the maid before our first kiss?" Julia asked him, meeting his eyes across the room. He hated the pain he read within hers and wished things could be different, but they were not. Life was not always easy. His certainly had not been.

"Before our kiss, but," he said, striding to the bed and kneeling at its side, "I have not kissed another since my lips touched yours. I could not. No one intoxicated my mind as much as you did, and when I married Freya's mama, I thought my life over. That I would have to stand aside and watch you wed one day, and my heart would wither and die." He cringed, hating that he sounded cruel and uncaring toward Freya's mama, but there was never love between them, and they had only been intimate the one time. "I never wished Freya's mama to die, never that. I made peace that she was the marchioness and my life would be with her and Freya. But I will not deny that having a second chance with you, falling in love with you all over again, and marrying you, was the greatest moment of my life. I love you so much, Julia. Please tell me you forgive me. Please say you love me still and that you will never run from me again. I could not bear it."

.   .   .

Julia stared at Cyrus, her heart thumping hard in her chest. He stared at her, his eyes glistening with unshed tears, and she knew her walls were crumbling, that she could not hate him as she wanted to.

She could not hate him any more than she could hate the sweet little girl above stairs asleep in the nursery. "I think it honorable you married Freya's mama, even if I do not think sleeping with a maid is acceptable." She paused, needing to ask a question that had been tormenting her for three days now. "Tell me this, and please do not lie. Let me know if there are any female servants under our employ with whom you have been intimate. I could not bear that."

He shook his head, clasping her hands. "No, none. Freya's mama worked at the Scottish estate, and it was only one night. Sleeping with my staff has never been a habit of mine. I'm so sorry, Julia. Please forgive me."

She reached out, clasping his jaw. "Do not ever lie or keep anything from me again, Cyrus. I may not be so forgiving next time," she stated, needing him to know that above anything, she did not want any untruths to be between them. "If we're to bring up Freya without any shadow following her about over her parentage, we must be a united front, and that means nothing between us, no secrets, nothing."

He nodded, his eyes beseeching her to allow him back in her heart. "I promise, Julia. I will do anything, but please do not forsake me. You're all I want. You're all I've ever wanted. I was just too blind and foolish to realize it until Perry made me see that I could lose you for a second time. I could not stand such a thing. I love you so much," he said.

Julia reached for him, and he came over her, kissing her

deep and long. They tumbled onto the bed, their need, their love holding them together.

Cyrus pulled back, staring at her. "Tell me you love me. That you forgive me. That tonight, right here and now, is the start of our forever," he demanded, his hand reaching down to drag her shift along her leg.

She grinned up at him, remaining silent a moment before he tickled her waist, and she relented. "Very well, I forgive you for being a foolish idiot, but I also thank you for giving me Freya. She's adorable, and I believe I already love her more than you, which is your fault."

He laughed, growling and kissing her neck, breasts, jaw, cheeks, wherever he could reach. "You are too marvelous for words. How did I ever get so fortunate?" he asked, meeting her eyes.

Julia wrapped her legs about his hips, bringing his delectable mouth down to hers. "I believe that has something to do with a debutante seducing a rake at her sister's ball and ruining him for anyone else," she answered, grinning.

"I am ruined, that is for sure. And yours, forever yours."

"As I am yours," she said, taking his lips and losing herself in his arms, his passion and love.

Always.

EPILOGUE

The Season, London 1824

J
ulia stood alongside Cyrus and watched as their daughter Lady Freya Chilsten started down the stairs in their London town house, presenting herself to the *ton*, who stood watching in awe as the Marquess of Chilsten presented his firstborn to the marriage mart.

Tears pooled in Julia's eyes, and she reached for her handkerchief, dabbing her eyes at the picture of beauty and grace that all but floated down the staircase. Images of a little toddler climbing down those stairs, but backward, when she was too young to walk down frontways floated through her mind. Or the many hours they had played with dolls and rode horses for fun, not to promenade and show-case her beauty and loveliness to those who would seek to make her their wife.

How had it been eighteen years since her birth? She was a woman now. Ready to embark on her life, love and be loved, just as Julia had the privilege of these many years with her father.

"Mama, the gown is exquisite. Thank you for the ball. For everything," Freya said, smiling and lighting up her heart along with the room.

Julia pulled her into an embrace. "You are too beautiful for words. I love you, my darling. Enjoy your night."

"Oh, I will," she said, all but bouncing on the spot before her friends claimed her, and they were lost in the throng of guests.

Cyrus came up to her, wrapping his arm around her waist. "You look as beautiful tonight as the night we first met. Care to take a walk out into the darkened gardens and relive delectable old times?" he asked her, his wicked grin still weakening her knees.

She pushed against him, chuckling. "Later, we will. I promise."

He escorted her farther into the ballroom, handing her a glass of champagne as they watched Freya be asked to dance by Lord Bailey, a young gentleman new to his earldom. Julia glanced at Cyrus and noted the small frown between his eyes.

"What are you thinking?" she asked him, curious.

"Do you think Lord Bailey's hand is a little low on Freya's back? I think I should intervene," he said, taking a step toward their daughter.

"You will not," Julia said, pulling him back and forcing down a laugh. "His hand is perfectly respectable. Now, if Freya were dancing with a man like you once were, then yes, we would have cause for concern, but she is not. I'm friends with the Dowager Countess of Bailey, and his lordship is sweet and kind. Do not think everyone is a rake such as you were," she reminded him, grinning.

"Hmm," he said, his tone unconvinced. "If I recall, you enjoyed my rakish wiles."

She slipped her hand down his back, squeezing his bottom and thankful they had a wall at their back. "Still do, my lord," she said, raising one brow.

He groaned, wrenching her closer still. "Likewise, wife," he said before looking about them and dragging her from the room.

"What are you doing?" she asked through her laughter.

"Taking you down memory lane," he said, finding a quiet, darkened corner of the terrace.

"Really?" she replied. "Did we not go down memory lane last night, too?" she queried.

He shrugged, pulling her onto his lap after finding the bench Julia had strategically placed there many years ago. "Well, one can never look back at such enjoyable times without doing so often."

Julia wrapped her arms around his neck, kissing him. "I wholeheartedly agree," she said, taking his lips again and losing herself in his arms. Losing herself in the love he'd graced her with all their married life. A life full of love and wonder, of milestones and wonderful children. A life well-lived.

Together.

Dear Reader,

Thank you for taking the time to read *Speak of the Duke*! I hope you enjoyed the third book in my Wayward Woodvilles series!

I'm so thankful for my readers support. If you're able, I would appreciate an honest review of *Speak of the Duke*. As they say, feed an author, leave a review!

Alternatively, you can keep in contact with me by visiting my website, subscribing to my newsletter or following me online. You can contact me at <u>www.-tamaragill.com</u>.

Tamara Gill

THE WAYWARD WOODVILLES

Series starts Feb, 2022
Pre-order your copy today!

DON'T MISS TAMARA'S OTHER ROMANCE SERIES

The Wayward Woodvilles

A Duke of a Time

On a Wild Duke Chase

Speak of the Duke

Every Duke has a Silver Lining

One Day my Duke Will Come

Surrender to the Duke

My Reckless Earl

Brazen Rogue

The Notorious Lord Sin

Wicked in My Bed

Royal House of Atharia

To Dream of You

A Royal Proposition

Forever My Princess

League of Unweddable Gentlemen

Tempt Me, Your Grace

Hellion at Heart

Dare to be Scandalous

To Be Wicked With You

Kiss Me, Duke

The Marquess is Mine

Kiss the Wallflower

A Midsummer Kiss

A Kiss at Mistletoe

A Kiss in Spring

To Fall For a Kiss

A Duke's Wild Kiss

To Kiss a Highland Rose

Lords of London

To Bedevil a Duke

To Madden a Marquess

To Tempt an Earl

To Vex a Viscount

To Dare a Duchess

To Marry a Marchioness

To Marry a Rogue

Only an Earl Will Do

Only a Duke Will Do

Only a Viscount Will Do

Only a Marquess Will Do

Only a Lady Will Do

A Time Traveler's Highland Love

To Conquer a Scot

To Save a Savage Scot

To Win a Highland Scot

A Stolen Season

A Stolen Season

A Stolen Season: Bath

A Stolen Season: London

Scandalous London

A Gentleman's Promise

A Captain's Order

A Marriage Made in Mayfair

High Seas & High Stakes

His Lady Smuggler

Her Gentleman Pirate

Daughters Of The Gods

Banished

Guardian

Fallen

Stand Alone Books

Defiant Surrender

A Brazen Agreement

To Sin with Scandal

Outlaws

ABOUT THE AUTHOR

Tamara is an Australian author who grew up in an old mining town in country South Australia, where her love of history was founded. So much so, she made her darling husband travel to the UK for their honeymoon, where she dragged him from one historical monument and castle to another.

A mother of three, her two little gentlemen in the making, a future lady (she hopes) keep her busy in the real world, but whenever she gets a moment's peace she loves to write romance novels in an array of genres, including regency, medieval and time travel.

Made in United States
Orlando, FL
23 October 2022

23773688R00104